Samuel French Acting Edition

LMNOP

Music by
Paul Loesel

Book & Lyrics by
Scott Burkell

Based on the novel Ella Minnow Pea
by Mark Dunn

Orchestrations by
Lynne Shankel

SAMUELFRENCH.COM   SAMUELFRENCH.CO.UK

MUSIC USE NOTE

Licensees are solely responsible for obtaining formal written permission from copyright owners to use copyrighted music in the performance of this play and are strongly cautioned to do so. If no such permission is obtained by the licensee, then the licensee must use only original music that the licensee owns and controls. Licensees are solely responsible and liable for all music clearances and shall indemnify the copyright owners of the play(s) and their licensing agent, Samuel French, against any costs, expenses, losses and liabilities arising from the use of music by licensees. Please contact the appropriate music licensing authority in your territory for the rights to any incidental music.

IMPORTANT BILLING AND CREDIT REQUIREMENTS

If you have obtained performance rights to this title, please refer to your licensing agreement for important billing and credit requirements.

LMNOP was originally developed by Breaking Bread Theatre Company and Third Coast Creative and was first produced by Goodspeed Musicals (Michael P. Price, Executive Producer) at the Norma Terris Theatre in Chester, Connecticut, from July 25–August 18, 2013. The performance was directed by Joe Calarco, with sets by Anna Louizos, costumes by Jennifer Caprio, lighting design by Joel Shier, music supervision and orchestrations by Lynne Shankel, music direction by Julie McBride, and sound design by Jay Hilton. The production stage manager was Nancy Uffner. The cast was as follows:

ELLA . . . . Lilli Cooper

GWENETTE . . . . Harriett D. Foy

EUGENIA . . . . Ming-an Fasquelle

TIMMY . . . . Noah Marlowe

PAYTON / LUG 3 / PERCY / MANGROVE . . . . Michael DiLiberto

ZACH / LUG 1 . . . . Kevin Melendez

SHUBERT / TAD / LYTTLE . . . . Aaron Serotsky

RUTH / LAGREER . . . . Donna Lynne Champlin

POPPI / LUG 2 / MIMI . . . . Talia Thiesfield

OTTO . . . . John Herrera

AGNES . . . . Stacie Morgain Lewis

GEORGEANNE . . . . Sally Wilfert

NATE . . . . Jared Zirilli

LUGS . . . . Kevin Melendez,
Talia Thiesfield,
Michael DiLiberto

H.I.C. . . . . Donna Lynne Champlin,
Aaron Serotsky,
Michael DiLiberto

THE COUNCIL TRIO . . . . Donna Lynne Champlin,
Aaron Serotsky,
Michael DiLiberto

WILLY / RORY / CREIGHTON . . . . Ryan Bauer-Walsh

CHARACTERS

ELLA MINNOW PEA – (18) Very bright, inquisitive, opinionated. Must be able to exude great strength and unstoppable, fiery passion. Contemporary musical theatre belt to a B.

GWENETTE MINNOW PEA – (40–50) Loving mother and wife. Loyal, sweet, and caring. Contemporary musical theatre mix, belt to a B flat.

GEORGEANNE TOWGATE – (30–45) Meek and quiet at first, with a fierce and passionate fighter hiding just under the surface. Soprano.

AGNES PRATHER – (30–45) Kind-hearted and loyal friend and mother. Slightly nervous. Contemporary musical theatre mix, on the legit side.

EUGENIA PRATHER – (11) Precocious and bright. Wise and extremely capable for her age. Contemporary musical theatre belt.

RUTH GREENLY – (30–50) Loving wife. Versatile character actress. Contemporary musical theatre mix, soprano. Doubles as the steely leader of the High Island Council, **LAGREER**.

POPPI MCGREGOR – (20–mid-30s) Strong and commanding. Good sense of rhythm, as LUGs march and speak in strong, rhythmic cadences. Contemporary musical theatre mix/belt. Doubles as **LUG 2**.

NATE WARREN – (early 20s) Scientist, student, book-smart, and compassionate. Contemporary musical theatre tenor to an A.

OTTO MINNOW PEA – (40–50) Devoted father and husband. Kind and gentle, with a dark and reckless streak hidden just below the surface. Baritone.

TIMMY TOWGATE – (11) A brat. Mouthy and rather simple. A bully. Contemporary musical theatre to a C.

ZACH O'DARE – (20–mid-30s) Character actor. Strong rhythmically. Contemporary musical theatre baritone/tenor. Doubles as **LUG 1**.

PAYTON EBERT – (20–late 30s) Character actor. Rhythmically sound. Contemporary musical theatre baritone/tenor. Doubles as **LUG 3** and **MANGROVE** of the High Island Council.

SHUBERT GREENLY – (30–50) Outspoken town leader. Stubborn and opinionated. Good character actor. Contemporary musical theatre baritone/tenor. Doubles as **LYTTLE** of the High Island Council.

PEABODY PRATHER – (30–40) Caring husband and friend. Contemporary musical theatre baritone/tenor. Doubles as **RORY**.

AUTHOR'S NOTES

All announcements from the High Island Council that come over the loudspeaker should be pre-recorded so as to facilitate cast doubling.

The cast can be expanded in size based on the needs and desires of the production by adding an ensemble. The ensemble can be used to fill out any instances where the script indicates "Nollopians," "High Island Council," or "Lugs." Specific speaking parts, however, should remain true to the character assignments indicated in the script.

In Act Two, as language has and will continue to diminish, bracketed ellipses [...] indicate a pause as the character searches for a "safe" word before speaking. A more conventional ellipsis, as indicated by three dots without brackets, is used to indicate a normal pause or interruption.

ACT ONE

Scene One

[MUSIC NO. 01 "OPENING ACT ONE"]

[MUSIC NO. 02 "LITTLE ISLAND"]

(It is early morning on the island of Nollop. The sun rises, the day begins. We see the **NOLLOPIANS** *starting their day.* **ELLA MINNOW PEA**, *a restless teenager, is isolated.)*

ALL. *(Except* **ELLA** *and* **NATE**.*)*

IT'S A BEAUTIFUL DAY IN NOLLOP

ELLA.

JUST ANOTHER DAY IN NOLLOP

> *(We now see* **GWENETTE MINNOW PEA**, *an elementary school teacher, addressing her students.)*

GWENETTE. Students, this morning we are going to start with a history lesson. As a matter of fact, we are going to focus on the history of our very own island home, Nollop. Can anyone tell me how our country was founded?

> **(EUGENIA**'s *hand flies up.)*

Yes, Eugenia.

EUGENIA. We seceded from the country of Atlantica.

GWENETTE. That's correct! Long ago our forefathers, led by Nevin Nollop, left the industrial giant of Atlantica, sailing toward what they hoped would be a better life. *(She refers to a large map.)* If we look at the map we see the huge country of Atlantica to our west and there we

are, that tiny little dot. But children, don't be fooled, for size can be deceiving!
OUR FOUNDERS CROSSED
THE SUN-KISSED BAY
TO CLAIM THE ISLAND
WHERE WE LIVE TODAY
THEIR COMMON CAUSE
A SHARED BELIEF
WHICH I SHALL NOW
DESCRIBE IN BRIEF:

> (*As* **GWENETTE** *continues, we hear the voices of the* **NOLLOPIANS** *filling the stage and sharing these common principles.*)

ALL. (*Except* **ELLA** *and* **NATE** *throughout rest of song.*)
COMPASSION, TRUTH
INTELLIGENCE, HEART
RESPECT FOR LIFE
A PASSION FOR ART
A FERVENT LOVE FOR WORDS
AND ALL THEY CAN EXPRESS

GWENETTE.
BUT MOST OF ALL, RESPECT
FOR ALL THE POWER THEY POSSESS

ALL.
THESE IDEALS WE STILL HOLD DEAR
THEY'RE THE BOND THAT KEEPS US HERE

ON THIS
SELF-SUFFICIENT
CULTIVATED
WELL-ESTABLISHED
INTEGRATED
LITTLE ISLAND
FLOATING IN THE SEA

GWENETTE. Now class, how does an island nation like ours and her people live? What do they need? The basics...

EUGENIA. Food!

GWENETTE. Very good!

EUGENIA. And shelter!

ALL.

THE COW GETS MILKED
THE CHICKEN, FED
AND WHEAT IS PLANTED
FOR OUR DAILY BREAD

THE BEACH IS MINED
FOR BRIGHT RED CLAY
AND BRICKS ARE BAKED
WHICH MASONS LAY
THE TREES ARE FELLED SO BUILDINGS CAN RISE
AND THEN REPLANTED FOR NEW SUPPLIES
THE PEOPLE PULL THEIR WEIGHT
WITH NO CAUSE FOR DISSENT

GWENETTE.

WE BARTER AND WE TRADE
AND ALL IN ALL WE'RE QUITE CONTENT

ALL.

SUCH A FINELY TUNED MACHINE
THAT'S RENEWABLE AND GREEN

THAT'S OUR
COST-EFFECTIVE
SELF-SUSTAINING
QUITE PRODUCTIVE
UNCOMPLAINING
LITTLE ISLAND
FLOATING IN THE SEA

GWENETTE. Now class, an easy question: Who is our island country named after?

(**EUGENIA**'s *hand flies up.*)

Eugenia, again...

EUGENIA. Nevin Nollop.

GWENETTE. Correct! And why was Nevin chosen to be our island's namesake? Someone besides Eugenia? Timmy?

TIMMY. (*Vaguely.*) He did something.

GWENETTE. Well he did a lot of things but one thing in particular that he is remembered for...anyone?

EUGENIA. *(Unable to hold back, blurting.)* He created a remarkable pangram!

GWENETTE. That's right! And what is a pangram?

EUGENIA. A sentence which uses all twenty-six letters of the alphabet!

GWENETTE. Correct again! And Eugenia, let's remember to raise our hand. Nevin Nollop created the sentence that we find on our currency, our flag, and most notably in the town square where Mister Nollop and his sentence are impressively commemorated in marble for all to see.

ALL.

> HE CREATED A SENTENCE, GRAMMATIC'LY SOUND
> UNIQUELY CONCISE AND UNHEARD OF AS YET
> EFFICIENTLY USING WITH LITTLE REPEAT
> THE TWENTY-SIX LETTERS OF OUR ALPHABET!

GWENETTE. A sentence that beautifully represents the potential of our glorious language, that we point to proudly as the motto for our country!

GWENETTE, EUGENIA & TIMMY.

> THE QUICK BROWN FOX JUMPS OVER THE LAZY DOG!
>
> > *(We now see the statue and a group of **NOLLOPIANS** staring up at it and singing with great pride.)*

ALL.

> THE QUICK BROWN FOX JUMPS OVER THE LAZY DOG!
>
> > *(As the **NOLLOPIANS** go about their days, we return to **GWENETTE**'s lesson. Their work illustrates her lesson: the well-oiled machine that is Nollop purring along.)*
>
> OUR HISTORY
> ONE MUST CONFESS
> IS QUITE A FINE
> EXAMPLE OF SUCCESS
> WE'VE FUNCTIONED WELL
>
> RIGHT FROM THE START

AS EACH ONE PLAYS
THEIR SPECIAL PART

EACH ISLANDER FITS INTO THE PLAN
CONTRIBUTING WHATEVER THEY CAN

IT'S EASY TO SEE WHY
IT'S MUTUALLY AGREED

GWENETTE.

OUR ISLAND HOME OF NOLLOP
IS A SPECIAL PLACE INDEED

ALL.

FOR WE FLOURISH AND WE THRIVE
LIKE A BUZZING, BUSY HIVE...

(A cacophony of sound and activity fills the island as everyone hits their stride contributing to the day's activities.)

ON THIS
SELF-SUFFICIENT,
CULTIVATED,
WELL-ESTABLISHED,
INTEGRATED,
COST-EFFECTIVE,
SELF-SUSTAINING,
QUITE PRODUCTIVE,
UNCOMPLAINING,
RATIONAL,
AND SYSTEMATIC,
SOCIALIST, YET
DEMOCRATIC
SLICE OF HEAVEN
CALLED NOLLOP!

GROUP 1.

THE QUICK
BROWN FOX
JUMPS OVER
THE LAZY DOG
NOLLOP!

GROUP 2.

ALL HAIL TO
NOLLOP!
ALL HAIL TO
NOLLOP!

GROUP 3.

NOLLOP!

NOLLOP!

(The day continues.)

[MUSIC NO. 03 "GOOD MORNING / THE 'Z' HAS FALLEN"]

AGNES & OTTO.

GOOD MORNING!

PAYTON & PEABODY.

SAME TO YOU!

GWENETTE.

HAVE YOU EVER SEEN A NICER DAY?

POPPI.

THE BREEZES BLOWING OFF OF THE BAY

ZACH, RUTH & SHUBERT.

JUST ONE MORE THING THAT MAKES ME SAY

ALL.

AREN'T WE LUCKY TO LIVE ON THIS ISLAND?!

> *(Before they can go any further, the unexpected happens. The "Z" on the statue of Nollop comes tumbling to the ground. There is a moment of stunned silence before one of the group, **PAYTON**, responds quite excitedly.)*

PAYTON.

THE "Z" HAS FALLEN!
THE "Z" HAS FALLEN!
WHAT A SURPRISE!
THE "Z" HAS FALLEN!

ZACH. Yes, we can all see that.

SHUBERT. How unexpected.

RUTH. How peculiar.

POPPI. Well, that doesn't happen every day.

PAYTON. It just tumbled! Fell to the ground, of its own accord! Isn't that something?!

ZACH. No need for hysterics, dear.

OTTO. That will need to be fixed.

PEABODY. What could it possibly mean?!

AGNES. Why does it have to mean anything at all?

SHUBERT. It's merely an accident.

RUTH. Yes, a fluke.

GEORGEANNE. Still, it is rather unusual…

PEABODY. I think it's an omen, a sign!

AGNES. Don't be silly my love!

> *(The **NOLLOPIANS** break into animated chatter, which **SHUBERT** eventually interrupts.)*

SHUBERT. Quiet! Rather than stand here fretting we simply must give this matter the attention it deserves.

RUTH. Exactly!

OTTO. Yes, let us take this matter to those we have elected to handle just such a situation. The High Island Council!

SHUBERT. Yes! To the High Island Council!

> *(The town square clears as the chattering crowd disperses.)*

ALL.
THE "Z" HAS FALLEN!
THE "Z" HAS FALLEN!

OTTO, GWENETTE, GEORGEANNE, POPPI, ZACH & PAYTON.	**SHUBERT, RUTH, AGNES & PEABODY.**
IS IT A SIGN?	IT'S A FLUKE
A PORTENT?	A COINCIDENCE
AN OMEN?	IT'S NOTHING AT ALL…

> *(**GWENETTE** sees **ELLA** lost in her book, lagging behind.)*

GWENETTE. Ella. Ella! Are you coming?

ELLA. What? Where?

GWENETTE. *(Frustrated.)* If you looked up from that book you might see that real life is happening all around you!

[MUSIC NO. 04 "ELLA'S PLEA"]

ELLA. I saw what happened, Mother…
THE "Z" HAS FALLEN!
THE "Z" HAS FALLEN!

> LET'S ALL BE REAL
> WHAT'S THE BIG DEAL?
> WHY ALL THIS FRENZY AND FUSS?
> HERE'S WHAT YOU DO
> SLAP ON SOME GLUE
> NOTHING MORE TO DISCUSS

GWENETTE. *(Giving up.)* I'll see you at home.

> **(ELLA** *is left alone.)*

ELLA.

> WOULDN'T IT BE NICE
> IF SUCH SIMPLE ADVICE
> COULD SOMEHOW PROVIDE THE KEY
> TO THE ENIGMA
> THE CONUNDRUM
> THAT IS ME?

> BORN ON THIS ISLAND
> THIS OCEAN-PLOPPED DOLLOP
> JUST LIKE THIS OVERSIZED, MARBLE-IZED
> NOLLOP
> OVERACHIEVER, I WON EVERY RACE
> HEAD OF MY CLASS
> NEVER LESS THAN FIRST PLACE
> BUT DEEP INSIDE THIS SUSPICION IS GROWING...
> WHAT'S THE PROFIT OF SPEED
> IF I DON'T KNOW WHERE I'M GOING?

> ELLA IS GIFTED
> I HEAR THAT A LOT
> AND SURE I LIKE "GIFTED"
> IT'S BETTER THAN NOT
> BUT ELLA, OL' GIRL
> JUST BETWEEN ME AND YOU
> OKAY SO YOU'RE GIFTED
> NOW WHAT DOES IT DO?

> BORED ON THIS ISLAND
> THIS ISOLATE ISLET
> SEARCHING THE SKIES
> FOR MY RESCUING PILOT

FINISHED WITH HIGH SCHOOL
AND NOW I'M PERPLEXED
WHAT DO THE FATES HAVE IN STORE FOR ME NEXT?
SOMETIMES I FEEL LIKE I'M HERE TO AMUSE THEM
WHY ELSE GIVE ME NEW WINGS
WITH NO CLUE FOR HOW TO USE THEM?

ELLA IS READY
TO PICK UP THE PACE
SHE'S TIRED OF MOPING
AND MARCHING IN PLACE
SHE SPEAKS IN THIRD-PERSON WHICH SHE CAN EXPLAIN
IT GIVES HER PROTECTION AS I GO INSANE

MY DAYS ARE SPENT BURIED IN A BOOK
PAGE AFTER PAGE, WHERE I LOSE MYSELF
WONDERFUL WORLDS THAT I DREAM ABOUT
WHILE I'M STUCK SITTING ON THE SHELF
HOW I WONDER WHAT IT WILL BE
THAT'S WORTHY OF A STORY ABOUT ME!

ELLA NEEDS ANSWERS
WHAT'S HER LIFE FOR?
SHE'S FED UP WITH CRAWLING
SHE'S READY TO SOAR!

HER FINGERS ARE CROSSED
THERE IS HOPE IN HER HEART
SOMEWHERE
SOMETHING
SOMEONE
HELP ELLA'S STORY START!

[MUSIC NO. 04A "TO THE PEA KITCHEN"]

Scene Two

> *(The kitchen of the Minnow Pea home. The room is now brightly lit with late afternoon sun and quite inviting. There are a number of rather elaborate dollhouses among the charming clutter. We find* **GWENETTE** *staring at the remains of a pecan pie. After a bit,* **OTTO** *enters.)*

OTTO. *(Entering.)* Gwennie is something burning?

GWENETTE. *(Showing the pie.)* Look. I lost track of the time and totally destroyed this lovely pecan pie. Where is my head?

OTTO. It's the waiting. It has us all on edge.

GWENETTE. The waiting?

OTTO. The fallen "Z"?

GWENETTE. How silly, I'd almost forgotten.

OTTO. It's been a whole day. What could be taking the Council so long?

GWENETTE. It must be exciting for the group of them to actually have something to discuss besides the time of the tides. They're going to milk it for all it's worth.

OTTO. Well regardless my Saturday has been quite productive. Close your eyes.

[MUSIC NO. 04B "A TINY TEA SET"]

> *(He presents a tiny tea set on a miniature silver tray.)*

GWENETTE. Oh Otto! A tiny tea set! It's petite perfection, it is!

OTTO. Hopefully these will prove popular at the craft emporium and along with the odd carpentry job will keep us afloat for the next few months.

GWENETTE. *(Crossing to a dollhouse.)* I shall place this new treasure right here next to the wee china plates.

> *(She takes his face into her loving hands and gazes sweetly into his eyes.)*

How do these clumsy hands create such tiny magic.

> *(They share a sweet kiss.)*

OTTO. Where's Ella?

GWENETTE. Upstairs, all day. I swear her mission is to read her way through the entire library from A to Z by summer's end.

OTTO. There could be worse goals, my love.

GWENETTE. She should be having her own adventures.

OTTO. *(Tongue-in-cheek.)* I knew we were asking for trouble when we taught that girl how to read.

GWENETTE. Oh Otto, hush.

> *(They are interrupted by a knock on their front door. It is **AGNES** and **EUGENIA PRATHER**.)*

AGNES. *(Entering.)* It's only us.

GWENETTE. Come in, come in!

AGNES. Isn't this odd? The waiting? I have spent the entire day alphabetizing my spice rack.

GWENETTE. I burned a pie.

AGNES. Aren't we a pair?

> *(The group is interrupted by yet another pair of visitors, **GEORGEANNE TOWGATE** and her young son, **TIMMY**. **ELLA** has also wandered back into the room.)*

GEORGEANNE. *(Knocking.)* Hello! It's just the two of us. Have you heard any news?

OTTO. Not a peep.

GEORGEANNE. I find it all so unsettling. I like every day to go along as planned, no surprises.

GWENETTE. Sometimes a bit of surprise can spice things up!

AGNES. My life could certainly use a little dash of spice. For our anniversary my dear husband just gave me a garden hoe and a yard of burlap.

EUGENIA. Hello Timmy.

GEORGEANNE. Timmy, Eugenia is speaking to you.

TIMMY. Hey.

EUGENIA. How are you today?

TIMMY. Bite me four-eyes!

GEORGEANNE. Timmy Theodore Towgate wait outside!

TIMMY. I'm sick of being bossed around! Timmy do this, Timmy do that... I hate you and this whole boring, stupid island!

(He storms outside.)

GEORGEANNE. I apologize, truly. You know I try my best as a single mother but every day I seem to lose him more. That little eleven-year-old boy is all the spice my poor life can handle.

*(**NATE WARREN** pops his head in.)*

NATE. Hello...? I'm sorry but the door was open...

OTTO. Can I help you lad?

NATE. It's Nathaniel... Nathaniel Warren?

OTTO. *(Not sure.)* Nathaniel?

GWENETTE. Oh my goodness! Otto, it's Nathaniel Warren! Come in! Nathaniel, come in this instant!

AGNES. Nathaniel Warren!

GEORGEANNE. Nathaniel Warren, my goodness!

GWENETTE. Ella, look! It's Nathaniel Wa–

ELLA. *(Interrupting, with sass.)* Nathaniel Warren, yes, I think that's been well established.

NATE. This can't be Ella... When I left you were a skinny little girl with pigtails and her nose buried in a book.

GWENETTE. Some things haven't changed.

ELLA. You're taller.

OTTO. What are you doing back in Nollop?

NATE. You are looking at an official graduate of the Atlantica Institute of Science.

GWENETTE. How wonderful! Are you here for long?

NATE. Hopefully for good!

ELLA. Why?

NATE. I heard word of an opening here for a high school science teacher and I'm hoping to get the job. My grandmother's house has been sitting empty since she passed so I figured why not blow off the cobwebs and settle down for a while.

GWENETTE. She'd have been so proud of you.

AGNES. Well, this is news!

OTTO. Welcome home lad!

> *(He exits.)*

GWENETTE. *(Calling after.)* Otto, dinner in an hour! Nathaniel, you'll join us?

NATE. If it's no bother.

GWENETTE. Good! Agnes, you'll stay?

[MUSIC NO. 05 "WOULD YOU LOOK AT THAT"]

AGNES. *(To* **EUGENIA.***)* Run home and get your father and tell him to bring the huckleberry cobbler since Gwenette destroyed her pecan pie!

GWENETTE. Make yourself useful and peel some potatoes.

AGNES. Aye, aye sergeant.

GEORGEANNE. Well, I must be on my way.

GWENETTE. Are you sure? At least stay for a quick glass of wine.

AGNES. *(Fetching it.)* Did someone say wine?

GEORGEANNE. No, I'm afraid I must get Timmy home before he sets something on fire... Good evening to you all!

> *(And she is gone.)*

AGNES. You know, I've discovered of late that most chores are so much nicer when accompanied by a big tumbler of pinot noir!

GWENETTE. Ella, could you go out to the garden and gather some tomatoes for the salad and perhaps a cucumber or two. Nathaniel, you'll give her a hand?

NATE. Gladly.

> (**NATE** *and* **ELLA** *exit, and the* **WOMEN** *immediately crowd to the window to observe.*)

GWENETTE & AGNES.
WELL, WELL, WELL…
WOULD YOU LOOK AT THAT!

GWENETTE.
MISTER WARREN
WHAT A NICE SURPRISE

AGNES.
HE'S TALLER

GWENETTE.
AND BROADER

GWENETTE & AGNES.
AND EASY ON THE EYES!

GWENETTE.
WELL HE'S CLEARLY WORTH A SECOND GLANCE

AGNES.
AND HE SURELY DOES FILL OUT THAT PAIR OF PANTS!

GWENETTE & AGNES.
WELL, WELL, WELL…
WOULD YOU LOOK AT THAT!

GWENETTE. We should be ashamed! A pair of middle-aged, married women drooling over a boy!

AGNES. Well we may be middle-aged and married but we're not dead.

GWENETTE. True. Or blind.

AGNES. Indeed. And he's hardly a boy…

GWENETTE. Oh, come away from the window!

> (*We move out to the garden with* **NATE** *and* **ELLA**, *who is still buried in her book.*)

NATE.
WELL, WELL, WELL…
WOULD YOU LOOK AT THAT!

OH MISS ELLA.

WHAT A SPECIAL TREAT
A PERSON
WHO'S READING
MY DAY IS NOW COMPLETE!
HOW IT LIFTS MY HEART AND MAKES ME SMILE
KNOWING SOME THINGS ON THIS ISLE ARE STILL IN
STYLE
WELL, WELL, WELL...
WOULD YOU LOOK AT THAT!

ELLA. It's just a book. I'm sure there were books in Atlantica.

NATE. Oh there were endless stacks of books on endless rows of library shelves gathering endless piles of dust.
READING IS SOMETHING THEY JUST DON'T DO
THEY JUST LOOK IT UP ONLINE
GONE IS THE SMELL OF A BOOK THAT'S NEW
AND THE THRILL WHEN YOU CRACK ITS SPINE

ELLA. Why would anyone want to come back to Nollop?

NATE. Why would anyone want to leave?

ELLA. But you've seen the world.

NATE. The world isn't so great.

ELLA. It's just so boring here, so slow.

NATE. You do realize that Nollop is wonderful, right?

ELLA. I get it. It's unique, we're lucky, I'm grateful. Yay.

NATE. You're young. You'll learn.

ELLA. It's just that I long for something more...passion, inspiration, progress!

NATE. Progress! I'll show you what progress brings. *(He takes out a cell phone.)* This little contraption symbolizes all that is wrong with that grimy world across the sea. This invention has turned people into idiots. Language is gone, people talk with their thumbs on these little keys, never looking up...

ELLA. *(Grabbing the phone.)* I have to see that...
WELL, WELL, WELL...
WOULD YOU LOOK AT THAT!

MISTER WARREN

THIS SEQUESTERED LAND
IS BORING
BROMIDIC
UNWAVERINGLY BLAND!
AND THEN OUT OF NOWHERE, UNFORETOLD
YOU PRESENT THE MODERN WORLD FOR ME TO HOLD
WELL, WELL, WELL...
WOULD YOU LOOK AT THAT!

NATE. You used the word "bromidic"! Do you know how thrilling that is?

ELLA. *(In awe of the phone.)* What does this do? How does it work?

NATE. Well originally its main function was to make phone calls but somehow that wasn't enough so now it takes pictures, clouds your mind with useless minutia...

ELLA. It takes photographs? How? Show me!

NATE. If you insist. *(He aims the phone at her.)* Say cheese...

ELLA. *(Confused.)* Why?

NATE. Oh, it's just something they say over there when they pose for a picture.

ELLA. *(Sincere.)* How interesting...
(She poses.) Cheddar!

NATE. No, not cheddar...

ELLA. Oh, sorry...
(Another attempt.) Mozzarella!

NATE. No! Not any cheese, just "cheese"...it makes no sense, it's...oh, just smile!

ELLA. *(A last attempt.)* Swiss.

   (He takes the photo.)

Where does it go? When can we see it?

NATE. The picture? Now.

ELLA. Now? No!! Let me see, let me see!

   *(**ELLA** and **NATE** are quite close. **GWENETTE** has returned to the window.)*

*(**ELLA** shows **NATE** the picture.)* Look, it's me! Isn't that something!

NATE. *(About* **ELLA.***)* Yes, look. Isn't that something.

GWENETTE. *(Seeing them sitting so close.)* Oh Agnes, look!
Isn't that something!

GWENETTE, AGNES, NATE & ELLA. *(Internal.)*
> THERE'S A SIMPLE KNOCK UPON THE DOOR
> AND THEN THINGS ARE DIFFERENT THAN BEFORE
> PROVING NO ONE EVER KNOWS WHAT LIES IN STORE!

GWENETTE & AGNES.
> WELL, WELL, WELL...

NATE.
> WELL, WELL, WELL...

ELLA.
> WELL, WELL, WELL...

GWENETTE, AGNES, NATE & ELLA.
> WOULD YOU LOOK AT THAT!

> > *(The lights fade as we transition to the next
> > scene.)*

Scene Three

[MUSIC NO. 06 "THE FORBIDDEN 'Z'"]

*(We see various **NOLLOPIANS** in their homes. It is the next day. A document has arrived at everyone's front door, and people are being summoned.)*

PAYTON. Zach! There is news! Zach!

ZACH. No need to shout, dear.

OTTO. Gwennie! At last there is word!

GWENETTE. Coming! I'm coming!

RUTH. Shubert!

PEABODY. Agnes!

GEORGEANNE. Timmy!

RUTH, PEABODY & GEORGEANNE. There is news!

GWENETTE. Well, what is it?

OTTO. Whatever it is it looks quite official.

> *(The various **NOLLOPIANS** who have just received the document proceed to read it aloud.)*

NOLLOPIANS. *(Reading.)*
OFFICIAL NEWS FROM THE HIGH ISLAND COUNCIL

POPPI.
AFTER A DAY DISCUSSING THE FALLEN "Z"
AND ITS UNPRECEDENTED DISLOCATION
WE WITHOUT DISSENT, AGREE

NOLLOPIANS.
ON THE MEANING OF ITS DETACH-ATION

GWENETTE, OTTO, AGNES & PEABODY.
NEVIN NOLLOP CAUSED THE LETTER FALL
IN A MOVE BOTH BOLD AND SYMBOLIC'LY BRAVE
AS A WAY OF SENDING A WAKE-UP CALL

NOLLOPIANS.
FROM HIS RESTLESS SLEEP FAR BEYOND THE GRAVE

GWENETTE. What?

NATE. They must be joking!

PAYTON. Nevin Nollop is speaking to us from the dead?! Really?

SHUBERT. They can't be serious.

RUTH. There's more...

> OUR BEAUTIFUL LANGUAGE HAS LOST OUR RESPECT
> SO A LETTER IS REMOVED, MUCH TO OUR SHAME
> AS A SIMPLE REMINDER OF OUR NEGLECT

NOLLOPIANS.

> AND IN HOPES OF REVIVING AND RELIGHTING THE
> FLAME

ZACH, PAYTON, RUTH & SHUBERT.

> BRILLIANT IN LIFE AND BRILLIANT STILL
> NEVIN COMMANDS US TO HEREBY ABSTAIN
> ABOLISHING "Z" AND RESPECTING HIS WILL

NOLLOPIANS.

> USING ONLY THE TWENTY-FIVE LETTERS THAT REMAIN

PAYTON. But wait! We are not supposed to use the letter "Z" at all?

OTTO. For how long? A day? A week? Forever?

PEABODY. What happens if we do use it?

GWENETTE. Will there be repercussions?

POPPI. Penalties?

AGNES. Punishments?

ZACH. What about me? My name is Zach! What am I supposed to do?!

PAYTON. Shhh, it continues...

> ANY QUESTIONS CONCERNING THE FORBIDDEN "Z"
> SHOULD BE SENT TO US IMMEDIATELY

GWENETTE, OTTO, AGNES & PEABODY.

> SO WE MAY CONSIDER WITHOUT DELAY

NOLLOPIANS.

> AND RETURN OUR DECISIONS IN A TIMELY WAY

GWENETTE. *(Reading.)* "Please join us tonight, eight p.m. at the Nollopian town hall where we will celebrate together the demise of this fugitive letter. Bring your dancing shoes and a snack to pass." *(Looking up.)* What utter nonsense.

GEORGEANNE. Nollop speaks to us from beyond...that's unsettling.

OTTO. If he *is* speaking to us I'm not sure I like what he's saying.

GWENETTE. Our glorious language *has* been horribly abused of late. I hear terrible grammar and sloppy bits of slang every day in the classroom. So perhaps an island wake-up call is not a bad thing.

AGNES. And it is an excuse for a party...and dancing!

NATE. *(A deeper concern.)* This doesn't feel right.

> *(As each* **NOLLOPIAN** *family rereads the document,* **ELLA** *slips out of her house for a private thought.)*

ELLA.
> SO THIS IS THE CHALLENGE
> WE NOW HAVE TO FACE
> SOME DUMB LITTLE LETTER
> WE SIMPLY ERASE
> AND ONE NEVER KNOWS
> IT MIGHT EVEN BE FUN
> SO ON YOUR MARK, ELLA
> THE GAME HAS BEGUN!

Scene Four

[MUSIC NO. 07 "GOODBYE TO 'Z'"]

(We immediately open to the town hall, dressed for a party. Glowing paper lanterns hang from the rafters and there is a large banner boldly proclaiming "GOODBYE TO 'Z.'" The entire island has turned out for the evening, and the mood is festive and celebratory. There is a large clock ticking away the hours. It strikes 9:00.)

NOLLOPIANS.

GOODBYE TO "Z"
ADIOS, FAREWELL
IN JUST THREE HOURS
WE TOTALLY EXPEL
THIS FUNNY LITTLE LETTER
NO MORE "ZZZZZZZZ"!

SHUBERT.

NO MORE SIZZLE

RUTH.

OR SNEEZE

PAYTON.

OR FIZZLE

RUTH.

OR FREEZE

PEABODY & ZACH.

IT'S FARE-THEE-WELL
TO TWIZZLE

AGNES.

AND TWEEZE

OTTO & POPPI.

NO MORE GAZING AT THE ZEBRAS IN THE ZOO

GEORGEANNE & AGNES.

IT'S THE END OF FROZEN PIZZA TOO!

ALL.

INSTEAD OF A ZEPPELIN

WE'LL NOW SEE A BLIMP
FLOAT FREELY UP IN THE SKIES
WE WON'T MUZZLE OUR POODLES
EAT SCHNITZEL WITH NOODLES
AND IT'S NOW A CRIME
TO HARMONIZE (HARMONIZE!)

 (The clock strikes 10:00.)

GOODBYE TO "Z"
ADIOS, FAREWELL
IN JUST TWO HOURS
WITH RELISH WE REPEL
THIS FUNNY LITTLE LETTER
NO MORE "ZZZZZZZZ"!

 (As the festivities continue, we see **NATE** *alone.*
 ELLA *approaches.)*

ELLA. What's the matter? Not in the party mood?

NATE. Hardly! I can't believe this is happening.

ELLA. Oh relax! It's just some pointless little letter. It's harmless fun.

NATE. And this from the girl who loves books!
JUST A POINTLESS LITTLE LETTER
IS THAT TRUE?
IS THAT ALL?
CAUGHT UP IN ALL THIS HULLABALOO
PERHAPS YOU HAVEN'T THOUGHT THIS THING THROUGH
NO LONGER TO TALK OF OUR TOPAZ SEA
OR THE BREEZE-KISSED SHORE
TO SPEAK OF THE AZURE BLAZING SKY
ON THE HAZY HORIZON, NEVERMORE
NEVERMORE!
FAREWELL TO BEAUTIFUL "Z"!

 (We return to the exuberant **NOLLOPIANS** *as*
 the clock strikes 11:00.)

NOLLOPIANS.
FAREWELL TO "Z"
ADIOS, GOODBYE

IN JUST ONE HOUR
WE FAITHFULLY DEFY
THIS FUNNY LITTLE LETTER
NO MORE "ZZZZZZZZ"!

    (**POPPI** *grabs the focus.*)

POPPI. It just occurred to me that we should all grab a partner! Quickly! There are only minutes left for us to dance our very last waltzzzzz!

NOLLOPIANS. *(Saddened.)* Awwwwww!

GWENETTE. *(Saving the day.)* No! It just requires an adjustment in thinking! Instead of a waltz, ask your partner for a three quarter sway.

NOLLOPIANS.

WHAT FUN!
A THREE QUARTER SWAY!
GOODBYE TO "Z"!

    (As the hands of the clock inch ever closer to midnight, the **NOLLOPIANS** *begin a spirited waltz. After a bit, the dancing is interrupted by* **NATE**, *who enters with a stack of official flyers.)*

NATE. *(Running on.)* Wait! Wait! Listen up! There is news from the Council!

    (As the dancing dribbles to a halt, **NATE** *distributes the documents among the crowd.)*

NOLLOPIANS. *(Reading.)*

OFFICIAL NEWS FROM THE HIGH ISLAND COUNCIL

OTTO. *(Continues reading.)* The concerns and questions you have expressed, after

CAREFUL CONSIDERATION, SHALL NOW BE ADDRESSED

ZACH. *(Taking his turn.)*

IF ONE SPEAKS OR WRITES THE LETTER "Z"
OR IS FOUND TO UNFORTUNATELY BE
IN POSSESSION OF ANY COMMUNICATION
CONTAINING THIS ALPHABETICAL ABOMINATION
THEY SHALL RECEIVE FOR OFFENSE NUMBER ONE

A PROMINENT MARK UPON THE FACE
AS A SYMBOL OF SHAME THEY CAN'T ERASE

NOLLOPIANS.

A SYMBOL OF SHAME THEY CAN'T ERASE

RUTH.

SECOND OFFENDERS, IF MALE, WILL RECEIVE
A FLOGGING OF THE BODY FOR THEIR DECEIT
OR IF FEMALE, HAVE THEIR HANDS AND FEET
LOCKED IN THE PUBLIC STOCK

NOLLOPIANS.

A FLOGGING OR THE PUBLIC STOCK?!

PEABODY.

IF ONE IS CAUGHT IN OFFENSE NUMBER THREE
THE VIOLATER WILL MOST SWIFTLY BE
BANISHED FROM THE ISLAND

NOLLOPIANS.

BANISHED

SHUBERT, PAYTON & POPPI.

IF THREE-TIME OFFENDER REFUSES TO LEAVE
THEN FOR THEIR PUNISHMENT THEY'LL RECEIVE
AN ORDER TO BE PUT TO DEATH

NOLLOPIANS. *(Did they hear correctly?)*

DEATH?

SHUBERT.

THIS IS THE OFFICIAL PROCLAMATION
NOW EVERYBODY BACK TO YOUR CELEBRATION

GWENETTE. *(Turning it over.)* Wait! There's an addendum…
ALSO WE FEEL IT MORE THAN FAIR
THAT ZACH NOW BE CALLED BY HIS MIDDLE NAME
PIERRE

> *(The news has cast a palpable pall over the group. It is finally broken by* **ELLA.***)*

ELLA. Look! It's almost midnight.

NOLLOPIANS.

FAREWELL TO "Z"
ADIOS, GOODBYE

BEFORE IT'S OVER
LET'S STOP AND DIGNIFY
THIS FUNNY LITTLE LETTER
NO MORE (NO MORE)
> *(The clock strikes midnight. With each of the twelve chimes, a "Z"-laden word is mourned.)*

PAYTON.
ZIPPERS

POPPI.
AZALEAS

ZACH.
ZIG-ZAG

RUTH.
ZUCCHINI

OTTO.
CREDENZAS

GWENETTE.
F. SCOTT FITZGERALD

TIMMY.
ZORRO

AGNES.
BAKED ZITI

EUGENIA.
THE WIZARD OF OZ

PEABODY.
ZAP

GEORGEANNE.
ZERO

SHUBERT.
ZILCH

ELLA & NATE.
NO MORE
> *(The **NOLLOPIANS** stare at the wounded statue with the missing letter and make their first tentative attempt to use their newly abbreviated language.)*

NOLLOPIANS.
THE QUICK BROWN FOX JUMPS OVER THE LA–Y DOG

(The lanterns are extinguished as the
NOLLOPIANS *silently leave the square.)*

Scene Five

[MUSIC NO. 07A "THE FIRST DAY TRANSITION"]

(We segue directly into the next morning: the first day of life without "Z." First we see **ELLA** *alone, trying on the abbreviated end of the newly altered pangram. Gradually we become aware of other nervous* **NOLLOPIANS** *starting the new day.)*

ELLA.

LA–Y DOG

SHUBERT, RUTH, PEABODY, AGNES & GEORGEANNE.

GOOD MORNING

BRAND-NEW DAY

RUTH & PEABODY.

I AM OUT OF SORTS

SHUBERT.

CONFUSED AND VEXED

GEORGEANNE.

I DIDN'T SLEEP

AGNES.

I'M SLIGHTLY PERPLEXED

SHUBERT, RUTH, PEABODY, AGNES & GEORGEANNE.

I CAN'T IMAGINE WHAT COMES NEXT TO...

(Loudspeakers suddenly descend into the town square. The first announcement of the High Island Council is heard.)

LAGREER. *(Voice-over from the loudspeakers.)* Greetings and good morning from your High Island Council. What an exciting day it is! The first with our newly abbreviated alphabet! You will notice some unfamiliar faces on our fair streets, uniformed mercenaries brought to our shores to be our very own Letter Usage Guard! So please give them a warm Nollopian welcome. Now, enjoy this beautiful summer day...but be cautious! That is all for now!

[MUSIC NO. 08 "RIGHT/WRONG"]

(There are three uniformed, rather imposing **LUGS** *suddenly present. The* **NOLLOPIANS** *make another attempt to start their day.)*

AGNES & PEABODY.

GOOD MORNING

RUTH & SHUBERT.

SUCH A DAY

I CANNOT COPE WITH MORE SURPRISE

PEABODY.

NOW WORD IS COMING OUT OF THE SKIES

RUTH.

IT SIMPLY MAKES ONE REALIZE HOW...

(Suddenly, an ear-splitting whistle is sounded, and the **LUGS** *immediately grab* **RUTH** *and mark her face with a dark, inky slash.)*

AGNES, PEABODY & SHUBERT.

WHAT DID SHE DO?

WHAT DID SHE SAY?

LUGS.

ILLICITABETICAL USAGE!

ILLICITABETICAL USAGE!

BLATANT DISOBEDIENCE!

COME WITH US

FIRST OFFENSE!

RIGHT! RIGHT! RIGHT!

RIGHT THIS WAY!

RIGHT! RIGHT! RIGHT!

RIGHT THIS WAY!

(As the **LUGS** *march off with the terrified* **RUTH,** *the crowd huddles.)*

GEORGEANNE, AGNES & PEABODY.

IT'S CLEAR THAT THESE ARE DIFFICULT DAYS

GEORGEANNE, AGNES, PEABODY & ELLA.

WE HAVE TO SIFT THROUGH EACH WORD AND PHRASE

I PRAY IT'S JUST A PASSING PHASE

GEORGEANNE, AGNES, PEABODY, ELLA & SHUBERT.
MAY THIS SOON FEEL RIGHT!

> *(A day has passed. It is now the next morning in the square. Again, the loudspeakers blare.)*

LAGREER. *(Voice-over.)* Good people of Nollop! As we start our second day of the new alphabetical order please gather for some important announcements!

LUG 3. *(Reading.)*
TO SHOW YOU THAT THEY LISTEN
THAT THEY CARE
THE COUNCIL AGREE AND THINK IT FAIR
TO LIFT THE RESTRICTIONS AND CAST ASUNDER
ALL PUNISHMENTS FOR CHILDREN ELEVEN AND UNDER

LUGS.
SO THOSE WHO HAVEN'T GONE PAST ELEVEN
ARE GRANTED A REPRIEVE FROM ALL KNOWING NEVIN

NOLLOPIANS & LUGS. *(Except **ELLA** and **NATE**.)*
ALL HAIL TO NOLLOP

LUGS.
OUR GUIDING LIGHT!

NOLLOPIANS & LUGS. *(Except **ELLA** and **NATE**.)*
ALL HAIL TO NOLLOP

LUGS.
WHO IS ALWAYS RIGHT!

> *(Again we focus on a group of **NOLLOPIANS** even more cautious then the day before.)*

RUTH, SHUBERT & GEORGEANNE.
GOOD MORNING

OTTO, GWENETTE, ELLA & NATE.
SUCH A DAY

GWENETTE.
I HAVE NEVER BEEN SO ILL AT EASE

OTTO.
I HEM AND HAW

RUTH.
I'M WEAK IN THE KNEES

SHUBERT.

    I'M JUST AMAZED HOW...

       *(Again the whistles and the ever-ready **LUGS**
       appear. **SHUBERT**'s face is marked with the
       staining slash.)*

RUTH, GEORGEANNE, OTTO, GWENETTE, ELLA & NATE.

    WHAT DID HE DO?
    WHAT DID HE SAY?

LUGS.

    ILLICITABETICAL USAGE!
    ILLICITABETICAL USAGE!

SHUBERT. *(Confused.)*

    WHAT DID I SAY
    SAINTS BE PRAISED?

       (He suddenly realizes.)

    OH MY STARS
    I SAID AMAZED!

       *(Immediately the whistles sound again and
       his face receives another inky slash.)*

    NO! NO!
    WHAT DID I DO?!

LUG 1.

    SAID IT AGAIN!
    NUMBER TWO!

       *(As the **LUGS** march off with the terrified
       SHUBERT, the crowd huddles.)*

LUGS.

    NOT RIGHT!

RUTH, GEORGEANNE, OTTO, GWENETTE, ELLA & NATE.

    WRONG!

LUGS.

    RIGHT!

RUTH, GEORGEANNE, OTTO, GWENETTE, ELLA & NATE.

    WRONG!

LUGS.

YOU CAN ONLY USE THE LETTERS
THAT ARE LEFT! LEFT! LEFT!

RUTH, GEORGEANNE, OTTO, GWENETTE, ELLA & NATE.

THIS FEELS ALL WRONG!

(We see **NATE** *and* **ELLA** *off to one side, alone.)*

ELLA.

IT'S CLEAR THIS MADNESS SOMEHOW MUST CEASE

NATE.

HOUNDED BY THESE SELF-RIGHTEOUS POLICE

NATE & ELLA.

AS WE COMPLY LIKE MINDLESS GEESE!
HOW CAN THIS BE RIGHT?!

*(Time has passed. It is another day. Tensions
run even higher. A group has gathered for the
day's announcements.)*

LAGREER. *(Voice-over.)* Good people of Nollop, we start week
number two with a most important announcement.

LUGS.

ALL BOOKS WITH THE LETTER MUST BE DISPOSED
SO THE LIBRARY IS OFFICIALLY CLOSED
BOOKS THAT YOU OWN MUST BE RETURNED
TO BE INSPECTED, DISSECTED, AND BURNED

(A book is taken from **ELLA***'s possession.* **NATE**
struggles to stop the **LUG** *from taking it.)*

NATE. Stop! Stop! This makes no sense!

ELLA.

BURNING BOOKS!
IS THAT THE THING TO DO?
ALL BECAUSE OF SOME DEFECTIVE GLUE?!

LUGS.

RIGHT!

NATE.

WRONG!

LUGS.

RIGHT!

NATE.

WRONG!
THIS ISN'T RIGHT!
WE MUST UNITE AND FIGHT!

LUGS.

WRONG!

NATE.

FIGHT!

LUGS.

WRONG!

NATE.

FIGHT!

LUGS.

WE ARE NOT WRONG!

NATE.

I DO NOT BELIEVE IN THESE LAWS
WRITTEN BY MADMEN
WHERE IS THE COURAGE AND SPIRIT
OUR FOREFATHERS HAD WHEN
THEY STARTED OUR WONDERFUL ISLAND?

(A shout.) Wake up, you fools!

LUG 1. Mister Nathaniel Warren you will cease and desist!

NATE.

NEVER! THE COUNCIL IS CRAZZZZZZZZZY!

(The whistle sounds as **NATE** *is grabbed.)*

LUGS 2 & 3.

FIRST OFFENSE!

NATE.

A GROUP OF INSANE ZZZZZZZZZZZEALOTS!

(Again the whistle.)

LUGS 2 & 3.

SECOND OFFENSE!

NATE.
SINCE YOU'VE MADE IT CLEAR WHAT MY PUNISHMENT
SHOULD BE
TIME TO FLOG ME SENSELESS FOR ALL TO SEE
AS A SYMBOL OF THIS INSANITY!

(There is a flurry of activity as **NATE** *is stripped to the waist and flogged. The* **NOLLOPIANS** *witness with horrified wonder. There is a cacophony of sound.)*

NATE.	**GEORGEANNE.**	**LUGS.**	**NOLLOPIANS.**
INSANITY!	ALL HAIL TO NOLLOP!	RIGHT! RIGHT!	WRONG! THIS
		RIGHT! WE ARE ALWAYS	FEELS WRONG!
FIGHT!	ALL HAIL TO NOLLOP!	RIGHT! RIGHT!	WRONG! THIS
		RIGHT!	FEELS SO
UNITE!		WE ARE ALWAYS	WRONG!

LUG 1.	**GEORGEANNE.**	**LUGS 2 & 3.**	**NOLLOPIANS.**
ONE!	HE IS ALWAYS	NOT WRONG! NOT WRONG!	HOW CAN
TWO!	RIGHT! HE IS ALWAYS	NOT WRONG! NOT WRONG!	THIS BE
THREE!	RIGHT! HE IS ALWAYS	BUT ALWAYS	RIGHT?!
FOUR!	RIGHT!	RIGHT!	

(The noise crescendos and finally the letter "Q" comes tumbling to the ground.)

ELLA. *(Simply.)* The "Q" has fallen.

Scene Six

[MUSIC NO. 08A "SCENE SIX / HYMN 326"]

(The Minnow Pea home. **SHUBERT** *and* **OTTO** *are seated, while* **NATE** *paces.* **ELLA** *is also present, helping* **EUGENIA** *with her homework.)*

SHUBERT. And so once again we wait for a decision from our esteemed Council who now hide behind closed doors refusing to face this mess that they alone have created.

OTTO. It started out so simply but it's gone so horribly wrong.

SHUBERT. So they should right that wrong now! The "Q" has fallen. Fix it and let's get back to normal.

NATE. Obviously this proves that what we're dealing with is faulty glue and not the insane orders of a man long dead.

SHUBERT. But there are people, our friends and neighbors, who now actually believe that Nollop *is* speaking to us and have elevated him to the level of a god. Unbelievable!

OTTO. Peabody waits in the town square and will bring us any news. Ella, you'd best get a move on. Your mother will be wondering where you are.

ELLA. It's all right. I told Mrs. Prather I'd skip choir practice and help Eugenia with her homework. Ella doesn't feel much like singing.

    *(***PAYTON** *and* **ZACH** *enter.)*

PAYTON. You are never going to believe what has happened to us! Horrors! Outrage!

SHUBERT. Oh no, what?

PAYTON. We have just spent an entire day in the company of the LUGs. My dear husband and I stopped by O'Looley's for a quick lunch and he stepped up to the counter and simply said, "We're going to share a…"

ZACH. *(Interrupting.)* Careful! Don't *you* say it now! Those damned LUGs are everywhere!

PAYTON. I wasn't going to! He said, "We're going to share a...a..."

ZACH. *(Helping.)* It's a round pie with meat and cheese...

PAYTON. Served in slices...

EUGENIA. *(Helpful.)* Pizza!

OTTO. Careful, Eugenia!

EUGENIA. It's okay. I'm only eleven.

> *(***ELLA** *escorts* **EUGENIA** *to a separate room to protect her young ears.)*

OTTO. Ah, to be a child again and free from these laws.

ZACH. Two illegal letters in one little word. Tomorrow I am to be officially flogged!

PAYTON. Flogged! How barbarian.

NATE. *(To* **ZACH.***)* You'll really enjoy it. It's great fun.

PAYTON. Also we were reminded that his name is now Pierre.

ZACH. I just don't feel like a Pierre.

PAYTON. And they ransacked our home and confiscated our monogrammed towels!

ZACH. And did you hear? A handful of islanders have committed a third offense and are now officially banished!

SHUBERT. I am only one offense away from joining them.

ZACH. As am I!

NATE. As well as me.

ZACH. They were taken to the docks...

PAYTON. Forced to empty their pockets to pay for their own passage...

ZACH. And tossed on the next outbound ship.

PAYTON. With the warning that a return to Nollop would result in their immediate execution!

SHUBERT. This has gone too far. All because of an innocent letter.

ZACH. People are packing up and leaving the island of their own free will.

SHUBERT. Who can blame them?

PAYTON. If this madness continues we should all just pack up and go!

OTTO. Honestly? You're going to leave your life, your friends, all that you know and sail off into the unknown? It's not so simple to leave your home.

NATE. And I just got back! Our roots are deep within this island. No, we will weather this storm and hope for its quick passing.

OTTO. *(Breaking the tension.)* Gentlemen, perhaps a game of cards to lighten the mood.

> *(He offers chairs to the newcomers.)*

Payton... Pierre...

> *(As the **MEN** settle into their game, we shift to the choir loft of the local chapel where the **WOMEN** have gathered for their weekly practice. **RUTH** leads them.)*

RUTH. Ladies, Hymn 326, "Marching Onward, Ever Onward."

CHOIR.
> EV'RY HUMAN TIE MAY PERISH
> FRIEND TO FRIEND UNFAITHFUL BE
> EV'RY COMFORT THAT I CHERISH
> SWEPT UP BY THE RISING SEA
> STILL I'M MARCHING EVER ONWARD
> MARCHING TO MY HEAV'NLY HOME

> *(An uneasiness creeps through the **CHOIR** as the forbidden letter is seen residing in the hymn. All of the **WOMEN** gradually drop out except for **AGNES**, who blindly sings onward, ever onward.)*

> *(Gradually dropping out:)*

> MARCHING ON
> TO GLORIOUS...

AGNES.
> ZION!

ZION AND THY
WONDROUS THRONE!

> *(A frightened hush falls over the* **WOMEN**, *who stare at an oblivious* **AGNES**.*)*

AGNES. *(Unaware.)* What? What is it? Am I flat again?

GWENETTE. No Agnes. The letter. You spoke it.

AGNES. *(Scared, realizing.)* But it's a hymn! Surely it's... I didn't mean to!

GEORGEANNE. And twice Agnes. Two times.

GWENETTE. *(Listening.)* Hush! Hush now!

> *(They all listen.)*

RUTH. No one heard.

GWENETTE. No, no whistles. No LUGs.

AGNES. I'm so scared! Two offenses! The public stock!

POPPI. Agnes, take comfort. You're with friends.

GWENETTE. Your secret is safe. Right, ladies?

GEORGEANNE. But doesn't that make us complicit? We're supposed to report those we hear abusing the letter laws. I don't want to be guilty by association.

AGNES. You would do that to me?

GWENETTE. If we start turning on each other what have we become?

GEORGEANNE. It just makes me uneasy, that's all. I want to do what Nollop would want.

GWENETTE. Nollop? Since he's dead I'm sure all he wants is some peace and quiet. Last I checked we only had one supreme being. How many gods are you listening to?

GEORGEANNE. All of them. I need any help that I can get.

GWENETTE. The right thing is to protect our friend. Her secret remains safe with us... All of us.

GEORGEANNE. *(Finally.)* I'm sorry, what was I thinking? Yes Agnes, of course.

> *(A comforting murmur is shared.)*

RUTH. *(Taking charge.)* Let us start at the beginning but from now on to be safe we use no words. We hum.

> *(The nervous* **WOMEN** *begin a wordless
> version of the hymn as we shift back to the
> Minnow Pea home.)*

OTTO. *(Laying down his hand.)* Gentlemen, a full house.

SHUBERT. Ah, nicely played. I was in desperate need of the
queen of hearts.

NATE. *(Chiming in.)* The queen of hearts. With no "Q" what
will we call her? The king's wife?

ELLA. *(Adding in.)* The king's better half of hearts?

NATE. Lacks a certain poetry doesn't it?

> *(A breathless* **PEABODY** *tumbles in.)*

PEABODY. It's only me. There is a decision!

OTTO. Yes...?

SHUBERT. Well, what is it?

PEABODY. We are to remove the letter "Q" from all usage
just like the letter that fell before.

NATE. That's the decision?

OTTO. When?

PEABODY. It is to be abolished at the stroke of midnight
tonight.

SHUBERT. This is absurd!

NATE. If only I could get a sample of the glue from one
of the fallen tiles. I have the tools to study it. Science.
Armed with cold hard facts we could end this madness.

OTTO. Unfortunately those tiles have been secreted away.

ZACH. And even if you were to wait for the next one to fall
there is a LUG on constant watch.

SHUBERT. We can't sit idly by and let this ridiculous behavior
continue. We must act!

PEABODY. A call to arms.

ZACH. A military takeover!

PAYTON. But wait, things could be worse. It is only a "Q"
after all. How often does one really have use of it?

OTTO. True, it is a rather funny little letter.

ZACH. We are lucky really that it's not something more necessary, right?

PEABODY. It seems best to just sit back and let this play out as it will.

PAYTON. We simply have to mind our "P"s and bury our "Q"s.

(There are a handful of cautious chuckles.)

ELLA. Listen to yourselves! Have the past few days taught us nothing?!

[MUSIC NO. 09 "IT'S THE CHOICE"]

THIS THING WILL GET THE BEST OF US
CONSUME US IF WE LET IT
I FAIL TO SEE THE HUMOR HERE
I'M NOT LAUGHING!
DON'T YOU GET IT?
TAKE AWAY THE CHANCE TO USE
THIS FUNNY LITTLE LETTER
YOU FURTHER IMPAIR OUR CHANCE TO SPEAK
WITHOUT HARNESS
WITHOUT FETTER

I'M TALKING ABOUT CHOOSING
THAT'S REALLY WHAT WE'RE LOSING
IT'S TO CHOOSE A "Q"
WHEN ONLY A "Q" WILL DO
IT'S THE CHOICE

YOU TAKE AWAY MY CHOOSING
TO CHOOSE WHAT WORD I'M USING
AND I LOSE THE KEY
TO WHAT IS UNIQUELY ME
IT'S THE CHOICE

IT STARTS OUT SMALL
A CRACK, A HAIR
BUT ONCE IT SPREADS
THERE'S NO REPAIR
UNLESS WE STOP THIS DANGEROUS TREND
IT SEEMS TO ME THERE IS NO END
NO END!

WE MUST PROTECT OUR CHOOSING!
THE GIFT THAT THEY'RE ABUSING
DIMINISH CHOICE, DON'T YOU SEE
AND IN TURN DIMINISH ME!
IT'S THE CHOICE!
CHOICE!
IT'S WHAT GIVES US OUR VOICE!
IT'S THE CHOICE!

    (The lights fade on the contemplative group.)

Scene Seven

[MUSIC NO. 09A "TO THE TOWGATE HOME"]

(We are in the Towgate home. **TIMMY** *sits alone with a schoolbook.)*

TIMMY. There are four "Z"s on this page and three "Q"s... Rip it out!

(He gleefully rips out the page. **GEORGEANNE** *enters and watches him for a bit, unseen.)*

No more stupid history! No more stupid geography! No more!

GEORGEANNE. Timmy? What are you doing?

TIMMY. I'm helping.

GEORGEANNE. Helping?

TIMMY. With the letter laws. It's our responsibility and our... something else... I forget... Our duty! That's it! It's our duty.

GEORGEANNE. Who told you that.

TIMMY. One of the LUGs.

GEORGEANNE. You've been talking to them?

TIMMY. Sure, I think they're great. These letter laws are the best thing that's ever happened to this stupid place. No more tests, no more reading, longer recesses. I hope the letters keep falling.

GEORGEANNE. I've never seen you so excited about something...

TIMMY. I turned in three sixth-graders yesterday.

GEORGEANNE. *(Really asking.)* Don't you feel guilty tattling on your friends?

TIMMY. Not a bit. You've always told me to follow the rules.

GEORGEANNE. That's true. We must follow the rules and listen to Nollop. *(She thinks for a moment.)* Go ahead, get back to what you were doing.

TIMMY. I'm not in trouble?

GEORGEANNE. Why would you be?

> **[MUSIC NO. 09B "WOULD YOU LOOK AT THAT – REPRISE"]**

You're only doing what's right. All hail to Nollop.

TIMMY. Sure… All hail to Nollop.

GEORGEANNE.

OH MY GOODNESS
WHAT A WELCOME SIGHT
HE'S SMILING
AND EAGER
NOT LOOKING FOR A FIGHT
THERE'S A CALL TO DUTY FROM BEYOND
AND IT'S ONLY RIGHT THAT WE RESPOND
AND IT GIVES THE TWO OF US A CHANCE TO BOND

WOULD YOU LIKE A HAND?

TIMMY.

SURE…

GEORGEANNE.

WELL, WELL, WELL…
WOULD YOU LOOK AT THAT

(The lights fade on the busy pair.)

Scene Eight

(It is evening in the Minnow Pea home. We find **OTTO**, **GWENETTE**, **ELLA**, *and* **NATE** *just after dinner.)*

NATE. That was the tastiest, the most delicious, the absolute finest meal I have eaten in many a moon.

OTTO. Mr. Warren, my darling Gwenette's culinary achievements are known the island over. No one can rival her crab cakes!

GWENETTE. Oh, Mister Pea...

NATE. *(Embarrassed, halting.)* Yes, and about the wine...

GWENETTE. Such an unnecessary gift! And on a school night no less!

NATE. I wasn't thinking. I didn't know that Mister Pea was... It was thoughtless...

OTTO. Not to worry son. I never let my sobriety stand in the way of anyone enjoying a fine Cabernet.

GWENETTE. Yes, six years sober, Mr. Warren! Isn't that wonderful?

NATE. Yes, indeed.

OTTO. Well, the gift of moderation was unfortunately not one I was blessed with and because of that I'm afraid that there were some dark days. I came so close to losing everything I hold most dear.

GWENETTE. But that's all behind us now my love.

OTTO. Yes. Also unsteady hands are a definite liability in my line of work.

NATE. You must show me more of your miniatures. They really are wonderful.

OTTO. Many thanks...and speaking of, a rather large order for tiny teapots, petite bunk beds and miniature moonshine jugs awaits me first thing tomorrow so off to bed I must go.

GWENETTE. I shall join you. The morning comes early and with it I must face a roomful of curious fifth-graders wondering why their world has been turned upside down. It calls for all my strength and so I bid you both good night.

> *(The pair exit. **NATE** and **ELLA** share a conspiratorial glance and listen.)*

NATE. Where are the tools?

ELLA. Shhhh! *(A whisper.)* Outside, hidden under the front porch. We'll get them on the way out...

NATE. We couldn't have asked for a better night...the weather is calm, the moon is full...

ELLA. *(Listening.)* I think they've settled in.

NATE. Let's go!

ELLA. And we're off!

[MUSIC NO. 09C "TO THE STATUE"]

> *(The two slip out the front door. We transition to the town square and the statue. There is a lovely full moon. **LUG 1** stands alone, guarding the statue.)*

NATE. There he is, right up ahead.

ELLA. Right where he's been every night. Alone.

NATE. Okay, here goes!

> *(They approach.)*

Excuse me, LUG?

LUG 1. Me?

NATE. Yes. We hate to be a bother...

LUG 1. The name's Cecil.

NATE. Okay, Cecil.

ELLA. We were out enjoying the lovely full moon and we heard someone down by the Nollopian cove...

NATE. Near the beach...

ELLA. Yes, and they were blatantly using countless numbers of illegal letters.

NATE. It sounded like they were plotting something.

ELLA. Well, we don't know that...

NATE. True, but they were definitely using illegals...we looked for help but no one was around.

ELLA. We knew you'd be here.

LUG 1. Yes, every night. Same old thing. Staring at this statue.

NATE. Must be hard work.

LUG 1. I'll say. Difficult to stay awake, nothing happens... and lonely, no one ever comes by...

ELLA. You could really make a difference, Cecil, stop some illegals, blow your whistle...

LUG 1. *(Intrigued.)* I never get to blow my whistle...

ELLA. And like you said nothing's going to happen here...

NATE. You'd really be so much more useful at the cove...

LUG 1. You think?

ELLA. Absolutely!

NATE. But you should hurry, while they're still there...

LUG 1. Yes...

ELLA. We'll keep an eye on the silly old statue...

LUG 1. Thanks! I'll be back...thanks so much!

NATE. Hurry!

> *(They listen for a bit, making sure he's gone.)*

They're as simple as they look.

ELLA. I thought he was rather sweet actually.

NATE. Okay, it'll take him at least twenty minutes to get to the cove and back...

ELLA. Yes, we should get to work...

[MUSIC NO. 10 "THE THINGS WE COULDN'T SAY"]

> *(**NATE** takes out the tools from the bag, a chisel and hammer.)*

NATE. So we just have to chip off a letter, remove a sampling of the glue and we're good to go...

ELLA. Okay...

NATE. Right...

ELLA. But which letter?

NATE. It's only a temporary loss, a means to an end...

ELLA. Still, having to choose...

NATE. How about "X"?

ELLA. Yes "X"...that's good, right?

NATE.

> I WOULDN'T MISS
> TOXIC OR TAXES

ELLA.

> INDEED

NATE.

> BUT EXTREMELY
> EXCITED
> ARE WORDS THAT I NOW NEED

ELLA.

> PLUS, A MOONLIT EXPEDITION

NATE.

> WITH EXPECTATIONS EXTRA HIGH...

ELLA.

> IT CAN'T BE "X"

NATE.

> I FULLY COMPLY

NATE & ELLA.

> THINK OF THE THINGS WE COULDN'T SAY
> ALL THE THOUGHTS LEFT UNSAID
> SITTING STUCK IN MY HEAD
> THE THINGS WE COULDN'T SAY

NATE. What about "L"?

ELLA. "L"? Well, let's see...

> I WOULDN'T MISS
> LONELY

NATE.

> OR LOSER WITH THE BLUES

ELLA.

> BUT LIGHT-HEADED

NATE.

    LIKE-MINDED

NATE & ELLA.

    I FIND THAT I NOW USE

ELLA.

    AND A LEARNED LAD WITH DIMPLES

NATE.

    MY FEARLESS LITTLE LOVELY LAMB

ELLA.

    IT CAN'T BE "L"

NATE.

    YOU'RE CERTAIN?

ELLA.

    I AM

NATE & ELLA.

    THINK OF THE THINGS WE COULDN'T SAY
    TIMES WE'D STARE INTO SPACE
    AS WE SEARCH TO REPLACE
    THE THINGS WE COULDN'T SAY

NATE. What was I thinking? Of course it can't be "L." I'd lose one of my favorite new words.

ELLA. What's that? Lolly-gag? La-di-dah?

NATE. No.

ELLA. Well, what *is* this favorite new word of yours?

NATE. Ella.

    (They share a sweet smile.)

ELLA. How about "F."

NATE. Never...

    FEELINGS...FLIRTING...FLABBERGAST...

ELLA.

    FASCINATION...FALLING FAST...

NATE.

    "M"?

ELLA. No.

    MOONLIGHT...MAGIC...

NATE.

"B"?

ELLA.

BEGINNINGS...

NATE.

BLISS...

ELLA.

"C"?

NATE.

COMING CLOSER...

ELLA.

"K"?

NATE.

KARMA...

NATE & ELLA.

KISMET...

KISS

> *(The pair share a lovely and passionate kiss under the full moon.)*

ELLA. Definitely not "K"...to finally kiss someone and not be able to talk about it?

NATE. To not be able to ask for more...as in "kindly kiss me again"...

> *(The two kiss again.)*

ELLA. Nope, not "K."

NATE. Cecil will be returning soon...

ELLA. We really should get back to the task at hand...

NATE. Yes...

ELLA. How about "J"?

NATE. "J"?

ELLA. I could do without "jaded" or "jealousy" or "judgement"...

NATE. But we would lose "joy" and "jubilation" and "banjo"...

ELLA. Well of course there are things we're going to lose! That's the point, we need them all!

(Pause.)

Did you say "banjo"?

NATE. Yes. I happen to play.

ELLA. There's so much to learn about you!

NATE. And you!

ELLA. I want to tell you everything!

NATE. I want to share it all!

NATE & ELLA.

SO MANY THINGS I LONG TO SAY
THINGS I NEED TO EXPRESS
THOUGHTS I WANT TO CONFESS
THE THINGS WE'RE LEARNING TO...
THE THINGS WE'RE YEARNING TO...
THE THINGS WE COULDN'T SAY

ELLA. So, "J" then? You don't have to say "banjo" to play it, right?

NATE. True. We could lose "J" for a little while...

ELLA. Jolly good.

(The two share a sweet kiss silhouetted by the glowing moon.)

Scene Nine

[MUSIC NO. 11 "ANOTHER DAY IN NOLLOP / ACT ONE FINALE"]

(The next morning in Nollop. We see various **NOLLOPIANS** *in various locations going about the day.)*

ALL.

> IT'S ANOTHER DAY IN NOLLOP
> YES, ANOTHER DAY IN NOLLOP

GWENETTE.

> LET'S GET TO WORK NOW CHILDREN
> THERE'S LITTLE TIME TO WASTE
> BUT THINGS WILL BE DIFF'RENT CHILDREN
> THAT IS TILL OUR TEXTBOOKS ARE REPLACED

OTTO.

> PACK UP SOME TINY CHINA
> PACK UP A LITTLE SPITTOON
> AND FOR SOME DOLLY TO DINE
> A TINY FORK, A KNIFE AND SPOON

GWENETTE.

> NO BOOKS FOR MATH OR HIST'RY
> NO MORE TO USE THE GLOBE OR THE MAP
> SO TEACHING IS A MYST'RY
> PERHAPS WE SHALL ALL JUST TAKE A NAP

GWENETTE & OTTO.

> IT'S ANOTHER DAY IN NOLLOP
> YES ANOTHER DAY IN NOLLOP
> TRYING MY BEST TO SURVIVE WITH THE REST
> THOUGH I'M FEELING DEPRESSED, OUT OF SORTS AND
>> DISTRESSED
> MAKES FOR A TRYING DAY
> A VERY TRYING DAY IN NOLLOP!

> *(We move to the town square, where* **LUG 1** *is announcing his discovery from the prior night.)*

LUG 1. The "J" has fallen.

NOLLOPIANS & LUGS.

THE -UICK BROWN FOX -UMPS OVER THE LA-Y DOG!

> *(We now focus on* **AGNES**, **PEABODY**, *and* **GEORGEANNE**. **AGNES**, *with* **PEABODY**, *is terrified.* **GEORGEANNE** *purposefully polishes a silver whistle.)*

AGNES.

YOU MUST BE CAREFUL, SWEETHEART
BE CAUTIOUS PLEASE, I PRAY
I WISH YOU COULD STAY HOME, SWEETHEART
AND GO BACK INSIDE AND HIDE ALL DAY

> **(PEABODY** *kisses* **AGNES** *on the cheek and is out the door for the day.)*

GEORGEANNE.

DEAR NOLLOP, HOW I BLESS YOU
A NEW DAY'S TRULY BEGUN
WITH GRACE I HUMBLY CONFESS, YOU
SAVED THIS MOTHER AND HER SON

I'M WALKING IN THE LIGHT NOW
SO NOLLOP, I DO NOT FEAR THE DARK
YOU'VE GIVEN US NEW SIGHT NOW
IT'S OFF TO OUR DUTIES WE EMBARK

> *(We see* **GEORGEANNE** *and* **TIMMY** *turn in* **AGNES**.*)*

GEORGEANNE & AGNES.

IT'S ANOTHER DAY IN NOLLOP

AGNES.

YES, A SCARY DAY IN NOLLOP

GEORGEANNE.

DOING WHAT'S RIGHT BY ADVANCING THE FIGHT
HELPING THOSE WHO'VE LOST SIGHT FIND THEIR WAY
  TO THE LIGHT

AGNES.

FEELING SO BLUE BECAUSE SOMEONE YOU KNEW
HAS NOW PROVEN UNTRUE AND HAS RATTED ON YOU
MAKES FOR A SCARY DAY

GEORGEANNE.

    A CAUTIONARY, NECESSARY DAY

AGNES.

    A VERY SCARY DAY

GEORGEANNE & AGNES.

    IN NOLLOP

        (We now find **NATE** *and* **ELLA** *examining the glue from the fallen "J" tile. They are side by side, rather close.)*

NATE. This sampling of glue is the key! Our covert efforts are going to prove fruitful!

ELLA. How exciting!

NATE. So, to work!

    IT'S KIND OF YOU TO ASSIST ME

ELLA.

    IT SEEMS THE LEAST I COULD DO

NATE.

    ALTHOUGH THERE'S DANGER
    I'LL BE DISTRACTED
    BY BEING HERE SO CLOSE TO YOU

ELLA.

    YOU'RE CHARMING

NATE.

    YOU'RE EVER SO CLEVER
    YET STUBBORN

ELLA.

    AND HEADSTRONG

NATE & ELLA.

    TO BE FAIR
    TOGETHER THERE'S NO STOPPING US
    WE'RE SIMPLY A REMARKABLE PAIR!

        (The letter "D" tumbles from the monument.)

ELLA. The "D" has fallen.

NOLLOPIANS & LUGS.

    THE -UICK BROWN FOX -UMPS OVER THE LA-Y -OG!

(It is a new day. Confused **NOLLOPIANS** *huddle in the square.)*

PEABODY.

IT'S ANOTHER DAY IN...

(The all-too-familiar whistle sounds.)

AGNES. No! That's three offenses! You can't take him! Please...

(With a distraught **AGNES** *trailing, a* **LUG** *hauls* **PEABODY** *into the shadows.)*

RUTH. *(Cautiously.)*

IT ANOTHER TWENTY-FOUR-HOUR PASSAGE OF TIME IN NOLLOP

YES ANOTHER TWENTY-FOUR-HOUR PASSAGE OF TIME IN NOLLOP

(We are now back in Otto's workroom.)

OTTO.

LET'S GET TO WORK NOW OTTO.

THERE'S LITTLE TIME TO WASTE

WHY DILLY-DALLY OTTO...

(Again the whistle, and **OTTO** *is marked with two dark slashes and trundled off. We now see a nervous, skittish* **AGNES** *fumbling with a large roll of black electrical tape.)*

AGNES.

I'M THINKING OF EUGENIA

I'M ALL THAT SHE HAS LEFT...

MMM...

*(***AGNES*** places a piece of tape over her mouth and sits in timid silence. We now see* **GWENETTE** *in front of her class. She is quite shaken and very cautious.)*

GWENETTE.

TAKE OUT A PIECE OF CHALK NOW

SOME CRAYONS, PASTE AS WELL

LET US WITH MINIMAL TALK NOW
COLOR OR DOODLE UNTIL THE BELL

> *(On hearing her mistake, a well-trained* **TIMMY** *seizes the moment and blows his whistle.* **GWENETTE** *is immediately marked and tossed into the shadows. We then see an ecstatic* **GEORGEANNE** *smothering* **TIMMY** *with kisses and praise.)*

GEORGEANNE.

OH TIMMY, COME TO MOTHER
WE WILL BE FEARLESS, WE WILL BE BRAVE
WE'LL BE THERE FOR EACH OTHER
TOGETHER OUR NOLLOP WE WILL SAVE

NOLLOPIANS & LUGS.

IT'S ANOTHER...IN NOLLOP
YES, ANOTHER...IN NOLLOP

> *(We are in the town square, where a group of disgruntled* **NOLLOPIANS** *have gathered.* **GEORGEANNE** *sees an opportunity to express her beliefs,* **TIMMY** *obediently at her side.)*

GEORGEANNE. Nollopian sisters, brothers, why the long faces? Rather than giving up why not rise to Nollop's challenge to think creatively? It can be great fun.

SHUBERT. Fun? Are you insane?

RUTH. I'm not feeling much like rising to the challenge...

GEORGEANNE. Well, we have no other choice now, have we? So the sooner we all accept that, the better it will be. Try! For example, since we can no longer say the names of the...units that make up a week... Timmy, if you please...

TIMMY.

FOR SUNDAY

GEORGEANNE.

WHY NOT USE *SUNSHINE*

TIMMY.

FOR MONDAY

GEORGEANNE.

MONTE SEEMS CUTE

TIMMY.

FOR TUESDAY

GEORGEANNE.

I PREFER *TOES*

TIMMY.

FOR WEDNESDAY

GEORGEANNE.

USE *WETTY* AS THE NEW SUBSTITUTE

TIMMY.

FOR THURSDAY

GEORGEANNE.

YOU MIGHT ALL TRY *THURBY*
THEN *FRIBS* TO MAKE

TIMMY.

FRIDAY

GEORGEANNE.

OBSOLETE
THEN IN THE PLACE OF

TIMMY.

SATURDAY

GEORGEANNE & TIMMY.

WE BOTH THINK *SATTO-GATTO*
IS NEAT

>   *(A small group are somewhat convinced and
>   gather around* **GEORGEANNE.***)*

GEORGEANNE. See! Try it!

GEORGEANNE & TIMMY.

SUNSHINE, MONTE, TOES, WETTY
THURBY, FRIBS, SATTO-GATTO!

NOLLOPIANS. *(Joining in.)*

SUNSHINE, MONTE, TOES, WETTY
THURBY, FRIBS, SATTO-GATTO

>   *(Another group of frustrated* **NOLLOPIANS**
>   *remove themselves.)*

NOLLOPIANS & LUGS.
IT'S ANOTHER *FRIBS* IN NOLLOP
YES, A *FRIBS* THE THIRTEENTH IN NOLLOP

(They are interrupted by the falling of another tile.)

ELLA. One of the "O"s has fallen.

(The crowd is agitated.)

GWENETTE. An "O"? How are we to behave? There are four "O"s in the sentence.

RUTH. May we still use the letter?

SHUBERT. How are we to cope?

*(Suddenly we hear **LAGREER**'s voice over the loudspeakers.)*

LAGREER. *(Voice-over.)* Since one "O" has fallen yet three remain you are to cut your usage of the letter by twenty-five percent. All hail to Nollop!

NOLLOPIANS & LUGS.
THE –UICK BROWN FOX –UMPS OVER THE LA–Y ––G!

(It is now evening.)

ALL.
IT'S A *SATTO-GATTO* NIGHT IN NOLLOP
YES, A MOONLIT *SATTO-GATTO* NIGHT IN NOLLOP

(An announcement is heard.)

LAGREER. *(Voice-over.)* Fair people of Nollop! For committing a two-time alphabetical offense the punishment is clear. Let the flogging begin.

*(As the terrified, silent **NOLLOPIANS** look on, a handful of offenders, **OTTO** among them, are whipped.)*

LUG 1. *(Counting the lashes.)*
ONE! TWO! THREE!

(Lashes four through eight go uncounted.)

*(**ELLA**, **NATE**, and **GWENETTE** watch to one side.)*

ELLA. How can we watch this without trying to stop it?

GWENETTE. Ella, it is best to keep still. Tomorrow morning it's the public stocks for me. One more mistake for your father or me means banishment!

ELLA. I can take no more!

> (**ELLA** *breaks free and climbs atop the statue of Nollop. The flogging comes to a halt and all gather to listen.*)

Fair people of Nollop!
BROTHER! SISTER! MOTHER! FATHER!
HOW CAN WE WATCH THIS INSANITY AS WE BOTHER
TO LIFT NARY A FINGER TO BRING IT TO A HALT?!
THIS SENSELESS, SACRIFICIAL ASSAULT!
THIS LAYING OF LEATHER UPON INNOCENT BACKS

ALL BECAUSE OF THE RULINGS OF
NOLLOP-IMPOTENT EGOMANIACS!

> (*A whistle-blowing* **LUG 1** *grabs* **ELLA** *and tries to pull her down.*)

LUG 1. Stop at once!

ELLA. Why? I am not using any illegal letters! Stop me only if I break a law!

> (*Suddenly, the tile holding the letter "K" tumbles to the ground.*)

Look! The "K" has fallen!
IT'S GOING TO KEEP HAPPENING, TILE AFTER TILE!
LETTERS WILL TUMBLE UNTIL OUR FAIR ISLE
IS NOTHING MORE THAN A SPECK WITHOUT A VOICE!
OUR NEIGHBORS, GONE! BY BANISHMENT OR CHOICE
AS THEIR HOMES, THEIR PROPERTIES, ARE TAKEN OVER!
LIVES BECOME NOTHING! CAST AWAY, FLUNG!
ALL BECAUSE OF INNOCENT SLIPS OF THE TONGUE!
VICTIMS OF LANGUAGE!
OUR SWEET LANGUAGE OF KINGS, OF KNAVES!
SHRINKING!
HOUR BY HOUR, TAKEN AWAY!
IN MINUTES IT'S FAREWELL TO PRECIOUS "K"

KAPUT!

A RAGE BURNS WITHIN ME!
I WILL NOT LIVE IN FEAR!

> *(In counterpoint to* **ELLA**'s *tirade,* **GEORGEANNE** *starts an opposing chant of her own that is quickly adopted by some of the* **NOLLOPIANS**.)*

ELLA.

THIS IS MY HOME
NOLLOP IS MY HOME
NOLLOP IS OUR HOME

GEORGEANNE, TIMMY & LUGS.

ALL HAIL TO NOLLOP!
ALL HAIL TO NOLLOP!
ALL HAIL TO NOLLOP!
NOW WE RISE TO FIGHT!

> *(The* **NOLLOPIAN** *crowd is divided. Some take up* **ELLA**'s *cause with a chant of their own.* **GEORGEANNE** *and the others continue, the passion escalating.)*

NATE, GWENETTE, OTTO, AGNES, EUGENIA, RUTH & SHUBERT.

NOLLOP! NOLLOP!
TOGETHER UNITE!
RISE TO THE CHALLENGE!
FEARLESS WE FIGHT!

NATE, GWENETTE, OTTO, AGNES, EUGENIA, RUTH, SHUBERT & ELLA.

NOLLOP! NOLLOP!
TOGETHER UNITE!
RISE TO THE CHALLENGE!
FEARLESS WE FIGHT!

NATE, GWENETTE, OTTO, AGNES, EUGENIA, RUTH, SHUBERT & ELLA.

NOLLOP! NOLLOP!
TOGETHER UNITE!
RISE TO THE CHALLENGE!
FEARLESS WE FIGHT!
NOLLOP! NOLLOP!
TOGETHER UNITE!
RISE TO THE CHALLENGE!
FEARLESS WE FIGHT!

GEORGEANNE, TIMMY & LUGS.

ALL HAIL
TO NOLLOP
OUR ONE TRUE
LIGHT!
ALL HAIL
TO NOLLOP
WHO IS ALWAYS
RIGHT!

(As **ELLA** *pulls to the side a bit* **NATE** *addresses the impassioned mob. She observes.)*

NATE. We must save our home! This is happening *here*, not somewhere else!

ELLA.
SOMEWHERE

GEORGEANNE, TIMMY, LUGS & PEABODY.
ALL HAIL TO NOLLOP!

NATE. Unite in our cause! Fight for *something*!

ELLA.
SOMETHING

GEORGEANNE, TIMMY, LUGS & PEABODY.
ALL HAIL TO NOLLOP!

NATE. Someone has to stop this! Be that *someone*!

ELLA.	**NATE, GWENETTE, OTTO, AGNES, EUGENIA, RUTH & SHUBERT**.	**GEORGEANNE, TIMMY, LUGS & PEABODY**.
SOMEONE		ALL HAIL TO NOLLOP!
	NOLLOP! NOLLOP!	
	TOGETHER UNITE!	ALL HAIL TO NOLLOP!
	FIGHT!	
YES!		
NOW MY STORY		
	FIGHT! UNITE!	ALL HAIL TO NOLLOP!
STARTS!	FIGHT!	
	TOGETHER UNITE!	ALL HAIL TO NOLLOP!
		WHO IS
	FEARLESS WE	ALWAYS
FIGHT!	FIGHT!	RIGHT!

(With the mob at a fevered pitch, the curtain falls.)

ACT TWO

Scene One

[MUSIC NO. 11A "ENTR'ACTE"]

[MUSIC NO. 12 "THINGS CAN ALWAYS BE WORSE"]

(We open once again on the town square. Prominent is a pair of wooden stocks where **GWENETTE** *and* **AGNES** *sit, hands and feet confined.* **AGNES** *still wears the piece of tape over her mouth. Sneering* **LUGS 1** *and* **2** *keep a watchful eye. Ironically it is the loveliest of late August days.* **OTTO** *sits quietly to one side, fuming, lost in thought.)*

GWENETTE.

THERE'S BRIGHT BLUE UP ABOVE
SO WE'RE SAFE FROM THE RAIN
IN THE FORECAST NO MENTION OF
A HURRICANE
THE TEMPERATURE'S COOL
SO WE'RE FREE FROM THE HEAT
THOUGH THEY MAY BE IN CHAINS...
AT LEAST WE'VE GOT FEET!

OH!
THINGS CAN ALWAYS BE WORSE
WHEN YOU'RE FEELING AS LOWLY AS LOWLY CAN BE
YOU MAY BE THE MUTT BUT YOU'RE NOT THE FLEA!
SEE, THINGS CAN ALWAYS BE WORSE

OTTO. *(Venting.)* I will never be able to fathom it! Teachers ought to be exempt! How are you to teach? Timmy Towgate blowing the whistle on you! The little son of a bitch!

GWENETTE. Otto! Stop at once! Now sit, calm yourself. You cannot spare another offense. Sit!

OTTO. *(Leaving.)* I'm sorry Gwennie... I cannot watch this...it's all too much, too much...

GWENETTE. *(Calling after him.)* Otto! Otto! Where are you going?

> *(But he is gone.)*

That's all right. He simply has use for a bit of alone time.

AGNES. *(A mumble through the tape.)* Mmmmrh Ghhhh...

GWENETTE. What's that? Have you rethought? The tape?

AGNES. *(Nodding.)* Mmmmmhmmmmm...

GWENETTE. Fine! Let's see what we can manage here...

> *(She calls to one of the hovering **LUGS**:)*

Yoohoo! You there! LUG!

> *(The **LUG** approaches.)*

Be ever so helpful, please remove the unnecessary piece of tape from my sweet [...] amigo here.

> *(The **LUG** obliges.)*

There! Much better! Now I can see your lovely face.

AGNES. *(Painfully cautious.)* You [...] are [...] my [...] pal.

GWENETTE. You'll get the hang of this speech without letters. It gets easier! Now, let's see if we can get a smile...
WE'RE CAPTIVE, THIS IS TRUE
BUT IT'S SO NICE TO SIT
SO THIS TIME OFF IS NOT WITHOUT
ITS BENEFIT
WE'RE OUT OF THE SUN
WE WON'T WILT OR PERSPIRE
WE'RE NOT FOOLISH OR FRAIL
NOR FAINT OR ON FIRE!

OH!
THINGS CAN ALWAYS BE WORSE
THOUGH YOU'RE NOT AT THE FRONT OF THE CIRCUS, IT'S
CLEAR

YOU'RE STILL NOT THE CLOWN SWEEPING UP IN THE
    REAR!
SEE, THINGS CAN ALWAYS BE WORSE

    *(**AGNES**, filled with a bit of confidence, begins*
    to join in.)

GWENETTE & AGNES.

YES, THINGS CAN SURELY BE WORSE

GWENETTE.

YES, IT IS TRUE THAT MY LEFT FOOT'S ASLEEP

AGNES.

HOW I'M YEARNING TO SCRATCH MY TOES!

GWENETTE.

ALSO I HAVE A SLIGHT CRAMP IN MY SPINE
FROM STAYING IN SUCH AN UNNATURAL POSE

AGNES.

I WISH OUR FAIR NOLLOP WAS NOT IN THIS MESS

GWENETTE.

THIS UNREASONABLE, ERRONEOUS REGIME!

AGNES.

THESE PLUMMETING LETTERS

GWENETTE.

INHUMAN ABUSE!

AGNES.

SO TROUBLIN'!

GWENETTE.

SO TRYIN'!

GWENETTE & AGNES.

I FEAR I MUST SCREAM!
AHHHHHHH!

LUG 1. *(Approaching.)*

CAUTION! CAUTION!
PLEASE BE WARY
SUCH OUTBURSTS ARE UNNECESSARY

LUG 2.

ALSO, REMEMBER HOW THIS GOES
YOU'RE USING A FEW TOO MANY "O"S

(*The* **LUGS** *retreat as* **NATE** *and* **ELLA** *enter.*)

ELLA. (*In disbelief.*) Oh! Such a sight! I am so sorry Mother.

GWENETTE. Oh, we're fine! Having a bit of fun actually.

ELLA. Where's Father?

GWENETTE. (*Covering.*) He's...not here. I'm not sure where he is...

ELLA. (*With unspoken meaning.*) Oh no, he's not...is he?

GWENETTE. Shhhh, he's fine.

AGNES. Ella? My Eugenia?

ELLA. I thought it best to spare her this. I left her playing happily with the Greenly girls. I shall have her safely at our home for your return.

> (*The* **LUGS** *blow their whistles and point accusatory fingers at* **ELLA**.)

LUG 1. You! Illicitabetical usage!

LUG 2. Illicitabetical usage!

ELLA. What? No... (*Going over her last phrase.*) "I shall have her safely at our home for your return." No illegals, not a one.

LUG 1. (*Embarrassed, but firm.*) All right, but you must slow your speech a bit.

LUG 2. All of you!

ELLA. Too fast for you? Having trouble? Tough! We've simply gotten more proficient at your insane game. Put up any wall, we will climb over it. We will learn to converse with numbers! Sign language! Anything to stay in Nollop. You want us to communicate slower? I suggest rather that you listen faster.

> (*The* **LUGS** *retreat. After a minute,* **GEORGEANNE** *and* **TIMMY** *appear.*)

GEORGEANNE. Oh my, my...to see you both in such a state is most upsetting.

ELLA. You can't be serious...

GEORGEANNE. *(Ignoring.)* I have brought some freshly [...] pummel...ish [...] lemon [...] beverage. Perhaps it will brighten your time.

ELLA. *(Trying to remain calm.)* I can't believe you have the nerve to show your face here. It is because of you that this atrocity is even occurring.

GWENETTE. Ella, shhhh...

ELLA. I will not remain still! I have things to say!

>   (**TIMMY** *blows his whistle and points a finger*
>   *at* **ELLA.**)

TIMMY. Illegal letters! She's using illegal letters!

GEORGEANNE. No, Timmy, she is using no illegals...shhhh...

ELLA. Tell me, how are you able to be so heartless to those who at one time you were close to?

>   (*Again,* **TIMMY** *blows his whistle and points*
>   *at* **ELLA.**)

TIMMY. Illegal letters! I know she's using them!

GEORGEANNE. Timmy, no.

(To the others.) He's overflowing with the spirit of Nollop, that's all.

ELLA. Answer please.

GEORGEANNE. Ella, I was not heartless or careless but rather my motivator was love.

ELLA. Love? Putting innocent people in chains is your version of love?

>   (**TIMMY** *again blows his whistle.* **ELLA** *goes toe-*
>   *to-toe with him.*)

Listen, you little genetic tattletale, if you blow that whistle one more time I'm going to toss it, along with you, into the sea thus bringing your horrible little snitching career to an efficient close. Got it?

GEORGEANNE. Timmy, wait over there...chat with a LUG...

>   (**TIMMY** *obliges.*)

GEORGEANNE. I am sorry it was necessary for us to turn these two in to the authorities but it was obviously the best, the only choice.

ELLA. Really, why?

GEORGEANNE. Because they must be put on the right path before they are sent away. When one plays with matches, there is punishment, so that one learns before the house is set afire. Surely you see the logic in that?

ELLA. Of course, but one may argue that this house of Nollop where so many fools now live is ripe for the burning.

GEORGEANNE. Whether you agree with the law or not is pointless. It exists. Now, I am sorry that our performance has brought shame upon these two but we are, after all, each responsible for our own actions are we not?

ELLA. We are. So my next action is to tell you to get out of here. Leave.

NATE. Ella...

GEORGEANNE. I really must be going.
(She calls.) Timmy!

> *(She gathers her things and proceeds to exit, but not without pausing for a final thought.)*

It's simple. We all must follow the rules or pay the price. All hail to Nollop!

> *(As **GEORGEANNE** and **TIMMY** disappear, **ELLA** can't hold back and calls after them:)*

ELLA. Your son is a brat!

GWENETTE. Ella!

ELLA. A snitch!

NATE. Ella!

ELLA. I also hear that he's a slow learner!

GWENETTE. *(Laughing in spite of herself.)* Ella, enough!

ELLA. *(A frustrated cry.)* Ohhhh, that woman! What has she become? Unbelievable!

NATE. *(Changing the subject.)* So, we have news! We have a big afternoon!

ELLA. Yes, we got official approval to meet with the Council.

GWENETTE. That *is* happy news!

ELLA. We will turn this [...] topsy-turvy isle right again if it's the last thing we [...]

NATE. *(Cautioning.)* Careful!

ELLA. Achieve.

GWENETTE. May fortune smile on you both! Ella, watch your tongue!

> **(NATE** *and* **ELLA** *exit.)*

You see, Agnes! There is help on the way! Hope springing eternal!

GWENETTE & AGNES.
> WHEN YOUR LIFE IS A LEMON
> YOU'RE LIMPING ALONG

GWENETTE.
> SINGING THE SORRIEST, SORROWFUL SONG

AGNES.
> WHEN YOU GIVE UP THE GHOST
> YOU'VE GOT THIS GUARANTEE

GWENETTE.
> NEVER LOSE FAITH

GWENETTE & AGNES.
> FOR YOU'VE ALWAYS GOT ME!
> SEE

GWENETTE.
> THINGS CAN SURELY BE

AGNES.
> ALMOST CERTAINLY

GWENETTE.
> MOST IRREFUTABLY

GWENETTE & AGNES.
> WITHOUT EXCEPTION
> THINGS CAN ALWAYS BE...

> *(Suddenly, out of the blue, there is a rather loud rumble of thunder.)*

AGNES. *(Unguarded.)* A storm. Oh dear, dear, dear...

> *(The* **LUGS** *immediately blow their horrid whistles, fingers pointing at a terrified* **AGNES.** *They slash her face with a third dark mark.)*

GWENETTE.

THINGS CAN ALWAYS BE WORSE

> *(Another rumble of thunder as the lights fade.)*

Scene Two

[MUSIC NO. 12A "THE CHALLENGE / SCENE TWO"]

*(The inner chambers of the High Island Council. **ELLA** and **NATE** stand alone. The Council are hidden behind drapery and bright, blinding lights. Disembodied voices are all that we hear. Their voices are also slightly distorted so that their number and genders are difficult to decipher. **NATE** is just finishing up their presentation.)*

NATE. So, honorable members of the Council, to finish, our scientific analysis points us to one conclusion. Within a matter of months, perhaps less, all of the tiles will tumble. This is not the action of Nevin Nollop but rather the result of a simple scientific truth: the glue is failing. We appreciate your generous attention.

LYTTLE. Yes, we agree, the glue is failing. But we believe that the faulty glue is simply the tool that Nollop has chosen to communicate with us.

ELLA. But...

MANGROVE. The proof we must have is that Nollop isn't acting at all. Nothing else will suffice.

ELLA. Proof? How? We can't raise the man from the grave to interrogate him!

LAGREER, MANGROVE & LYTTLE.
YES, A PROBLEM PERPLEXING IT'S TRUE
THEREFORE THIS MEETING IS OFFICIALLY THROUGH

ELLA. I tell you the villagers are growing restless! If things remain the same I promise you they will soon be storming the gates!

LYTTLE. If you grow weary of our isle simply sail away to wherever you choose.

ELLA. Open your eyes! The country has been split in two, some crouch in corners, others blow whistles while pointing fingers...all because of the worship of a man who strung a few letters together! Is that really an accomplishment worthy of such chaos?

LAGREER. You believe it is not?

ELLA. I believe Nollop was probably a nice guy with a love of language. Nothing more, nothing less.

LAGREER. If his achievement is so common, so unexceptional then why not try it yourselves? Come up with a sentence of your own.

NATE. If we accomplish this?

LAGREER. Well naturally if one bests almighty Nollop by creating a sentence that matches his...

ELLA. *(Feeling cocky.)* Or a sentence shorter than his!

LAGREER. Then it proves your theory that he is not almighty but rather that he is merely one of us...

ELLA. Yes, so then you must remove the alphabet laws thereby returning things to normal. Correct?

LAGREER. Naturally.

NATE. Might you welcome such a challenge?

LAGREER. We may not welcome it but in the spirit of fairness, we must entertain it.

ELLA. Fine. What are the rules?

LAGREER. Well Nollop's pangram contains thirty-five letters. Yours must be shorter.

ELLA. Thirty-four!

LAGREER. Thirty-three!

ELLA. *(On a roll.)* Thirty-two! Let's bury this myth of Nollop forever.

LAGREER. Very well...we set the challenge at thirty-two letters.

ELLA. Fine.

NATE. How long have we to complete this mission?

LAGREER. Let us say you have until October 15, Nollop's birth anniversary. Which is about...oh, forty-five sun-to-suns from now.

ELLA. *(Inspired.)* So, here's to Enterprise Thirty-two!

NATE. Enterprise Thirty-two!

LAGREER. Enterprise Thirty-two. Yes.

Scene Three

[MUSIC NO. 12B "OTTO'S ARREST"]

(We see **OTTO** *wander into the busy town square. He is disheveled, distraught, and drunk, a liquor bottle in his tightly clenched fist. He looks up at the amputated statue of Nollop. After a moment of decision he plants himself firmly and with unflinching passion begins to sing.)*

OTTO.

THE QUICK BROWN FOX JUMPS OVER THE LAZY DOG!

(The **NOLLOPIANS** *in the square stop, crippled with the hearing of the illegal letters.* **OTTO** *continues.)*

THE QUICK BROWN FOX JUMPS OVER THE LAZY DOG!

SHUBERT. *(Emerging from the crowd.)* Otto! Stop! You must stop!

OTTO. *(Ignoring.)*

THE QUICK BROWN FOX JUMPS OVER THE LAZY –

(Before he can finish, there is a blare of whistles and a **LUG** *immediately hauls him into the shadows as the terrified* **NOLLOPIANS** *and a helpless* **SHUBERT** *look on.)*

Scene Four

[MUSIC NO. 13 "FAREWELL FAIR NOLLOP"]

(We immediately segue to Pier Seven. A group of sad **NOLLOPIANS**, *baggage in tow, are sharing final moments with loved ones.* **AGNES, EUGENIA, NATE,** *and the* **MINNOW PEA** *family are present.* **LUG 1** *addresses the crowd through a blaring bullhorn.)*

LUG 1. All those leaving Nollop for permanent expulsion on this first Fribs of September listen up!

Soon expulsion-people will hear their names. When that happens, register with the Ousting Officer. The banishment allowance of one suitcase is in strict observance! All other items will be eligible for search plus confiscation! One suitcase! No exceptions!

(We focus on **AGNES, EUGENIA,** *and the* **MINNOW PEAS.**)

AGNES. Is this really happening?

ELLA. It will all be fine. We'll watch Eugenia until your return.

AGNES. I am forever grateful. We have not the money nor my cousins the room for her to join us.

GWENETTE. You stay a spell with your relatives in Atlantica. At least you will be with your spouse again. Take comfort in that.

AGNES. Will you water my plants?

ELLA. Of course.

*(***LUG 1** *begins calling the names of those being expelled and the line proceeds onto the pier.)*

LUG 1. *(In rhythm to music underscoring.)*
TASSIE PURCY!

EUGENIA. *(Suddenly frightened.)* Mother, I'm scared! Please don't go!

AGNES. *(Struggling to remain strong.)* Oh Eugenia, don't…

LUG 1.

> AGNES PRATHER!

EUGENIA. No! Who will tuck me in?! Don't go!

AGNES. *(Pleading.)* Ella! Take her, please!

> (**ELLA** *grabs* **EUGENIA** *as* **AGNES** *is pulled away
> and shoved into the line.)*

LUG 1.

> CUBETTA LOUISE!

GWENETTE. Otto we have never spent a night apart…

OTTO. I know my love.

GWENETTE. How will I survive?

LUG 1.

> PETER CUMMEL!

OTTO. Ella, stay strong! Help your mother…

ELLA. Of course. No worries, Pop.

LUG 1.

> CREIGHTON O'LOOLEY!

OTTO. Nate, I'm counting on you to watch my girls.

NATE. I will Mr. Pea.

LUG 1.

> OTTO MINNOW PEA!

> (**OTTO** *gives last hugs and kisses and moves
> into the line of exiting exiles.)*

OTTO.

> GOODBYE MY WIFE
> MY DAUGHTER FAIR
> OH, LET'S NOT CRY
> BE WELL, TAKE CARE

NOLLOPIANS.

> WE'LL MEET AGAIN, THIS I PRAY
> WITH HEAVIEST HEART, NOW I SAY
> FAREWELL FAIR NOLLOP, FAREWELL FAIR NOLLOP
> FAREWELL!

> *(The departing slip out of view, leaving their
> families behind.* **LUG 1** *continues with the*

day's announcements. First we hear **LAGREER**
over the loudspeakers.)

LAGREER. *(Voice-over.)* Fellow Nollopians! Attention! Listen up!

LUG 1.

SINCE MANY HAVE LEFT OR ARE RELOCATING
THEIR HOMES ARE IN A STATE OF NON-OCCUPATING
SO THE COUNCIL WILL CONTINUE CONFISCATING
ALL SUCH PROPERTIES

NOW, MANY MAY FEEL THIS SORT OF CONFISCATION
IS SOME SORT OF CONSTITUTIONAL VIOLATION
BUT THIS CRISIS CALLS FOR NEW INTERPRETATION
OF ALL PREVIOUS LAWS

ALSO, ANOTHER "O" FELL FROM THE CENOTAPH
SO PLEASE CUT YOUR USAGE BY EXACTLY HALF

LAGREER. *(Voice-over.)* That is all for now. Have a lovely sun-to-sun! All hail to Nollop!

> (**LUG 1** *exits, leaving a group of confused and disgruntled* **NOLLOPIANS**.*)*

PAYTON. Our laws now thrown away! What next?

RORY. My home is all I possess, left to me by my father. Gone now.

SHUBERT. Stores are closing.

POPPI. Rationing of supplies, electricity!

RORY. Gone...

POPPI. Shelves are empty.

PAYTON. They will not be content until they have stolen everything in sight.

RORY. Gone. Everything is gone now.

PAYTON. My sister.

EUGENIA. My mother.

RORY. My father.

SHUBERT. Our very tongues.

ELLA. So we must now begin! Salvation is in our reach! Enterprise Thirty-two!

(There is a moment of confused silence.)

POPPI. Enterprise Thirty-two?

RUTH. What is it?

SHUBERT. Whatever it is if it helps us stop the Council then I'm all for it.

RORY. How are we to start this Enterprise Thirty-two?

ELLA. We create a sentence shorter than Nollop's then the Council will stop all of this insanity, returning our poor home to normal.

SHUBERT. It's that simple? So let's begin!

NATE. Yes, so as with any mission first we must gather our tools. In this case: pencil, paper, our brains…

ELLA. Plus our most […] valuable one: anyone who is age eleven or below.

[MUSIC NO. 14 "PENCIL TO PAPER"]

NATE. Let us start by forming a list of […] the units of language…

EUGENIA. *(Clarifying.)* Words!

ELLA. Yes! Especially ones that are short of length yet use a variety of letters.

(There is a pause as they struggle to begin.)

NATE. Why not begin with the ones we *can* say since they contain no illegals.

*(Slowly they begin to compile a list, which **EUGENIA** writes down.)*

ELLA.

SMART!

RUTH.

ENEMY!

RORY.

WALNUT!

NATE. *(Encouraging.)*

THAT'S GREAT!

POPPI.

SMALL!

SHUBERT.

>BEFORE!

PAYTON.

>SEVEN!

RUTH.

>EIGHT!

ALL.

>PENCIL TO PAPER
>WE'RE OFF ON OUR WAY

POPPI.

>TWIG!

RORY.

>FORGOT!

SHUBERT.

>CHUBBY!

RUTH.

>TWIRL!

ALL.

>STARTING A LIST
>OF THE THINGS WE CAN SAY

SHUBERT.

>FIVE!

PAYTON.

>BOATS!

POPPI.

>NUBBY!

RUTH.

>GIRL!

ELLA. Now, how about a bit more of a challenge? ...Things we *cannot* say or write since they contain illegals.

NATE. Eugenia, this is where you and any youngster below eleven become vital, crucial! All set?

EUGENIA. Ready Mister Nate.

NATE.

>THE OPPOSITE OF SLOW IS...

EUGENIA.

>QUICK!

NATE.
> I RUN A FEVER WHEN I'M...

EUGENIA.
> SICK!

NATE. *(To* **EUGENIA.***)* Write them please...
> *(To the adults.)* Remember the youngsters must say, plus possess, the illegals. We cannot!

ELLA.
> MY SWEATER FITS SINCE I BOUGHT THE RIGHT...

EUGENIA.
> SIZE!

RUTH.
> THE SUN IS SHINING UP IN THE...

EUGENIA.
> SKIES!

RORY.
> GUESS MY WEIGHT YOU WIN A...

EUGENIA.
> PRIZE!

NATE.
> IF I PUT YOU IN PERIL I...

> *(There is a pause as* **EUGENIA** *ponders.)*

ELLA. That's too challenging...

EUGENIA. *(Triumphant.)* Jeopardize!
> *(To* **ELLA.***)* I have a very advanced vocabulary for a girl my age.

ELLA. I'll say!

NATE. Now we form a sentence...

POPPI. How?

ELLA. We choose something from our list such as "enemy" then construct our sentence from it...
> *(She starts.)* The Enemy Will...

EUGENIA. *(Doing her part.)* Jeopardize!

NATE. Great!

EUGENIA. The Enemy Will Jeopardize...

RUTH. *(Excited, adding on.)* ...Us With Guns!

> **(EUGENIA** *tallies up the letters as the rest wait.)*

ALL.

> CHOOSING THE LETTERS TO TOSS IN THE MIX
> CREATING A SENTENCE FROM ALL TWENTY-SIX

ELLA & EUGENIA. The Enemy Will...

EUGENIA. Jeopardize.

ELLA & EUGENIA. Us With Guns!

EUGENIA. We've used nineteen of the twenty-six letters.

ELLA. Only seven letters left we have to use!

EUGENIA. *(Coming up with a word.)* How about "Quick"?

NATE. Excellent!

ELLA. Put it before "Enemy"...

ELLA, EUGENIA & RUTH. The...

EUGENIA. Quick...

ELLA, EUGENIA & RUTH. Enemy Will...

EUGENIA. Jeopardize...

RUTH. *(Thrilled, adding on her addition.)* Us With Guns!

ELLA. That only leaves four letters to use: "B," "F," "V," "X"...

POPPI. *(Contributing.)* Box!

SHUBERT. Six!

RORY. *(Putting it together.)* From A Box!

SHUBERT. Six Guns From A Box!

EUGENIA. *(Summarizing.)* The Quick...

ALL. Enemy Will...

EUGENIA. Jeopardize...

ALL. Us With Six Guns From A Box!

ELLA. Only the letter "V" is left!

PAYTON. Visit!

POPPI. Value!

RUTH. Vague!

> **(GWENETTE,** *who has been observing quietly, adds in:)*

GWENETTE. Vain. The Vain Enemy. That's even shorter.

EUGENIA. The Quick...

ALL. Vain Enemy Will...

EUGENIA. Jeopardize...

ALL. Us With Six Guns From A Box!

ELLA. That uses all twenty-six letters of the alphabet!

NATE. Now we total up how many letters are in our sentence!

ALL.

> WE REACH THIRTY-TWO, THEN OUR MISSION IS THROUGH
> OUR FIRST ATTEMPT OVER...

NATE.

> HOW MANY?

ELLA. *(The simple truth.)* Fifty-two.

> *(Their excitement gives way to disappointment.)*

POPPI. Fifty-two...twenty letters too many...

RUTH. Perhaps this is going to be [...] more challenging than we thought...

ELLA. It's only our first attempt! Let us remain optimistic!

SHUBERT. Yes, we must try. It seems to be our only hope.

ELLA. That's the spirit!

NATE. Now to your homes! Locate a youngster then start!

ELLA. We have no time to lose! Here's to Enterprise Thirty-two!

ALL. Enterprise Thirty-two!

> *(The scene shifts as the **NOLLOPIANS** begin the task of Enterprise 32. We focus on **NATE** and **ELLA**, who are busy with **EUGENIA**, who writes down the words that they pantomime. They are energized and intent. We also see **GWENETTE** toiling away, busy with pencil and paper in a separate part of the Minnow Pea home.)*

ALL. *(Except **NATE**, **ELLA**, and **EUGENIA**.)*

> PENCIL TO PAPER

WITH LETTERS WE TRY
CROSS OUT THE "T"
MOVE THE "P"
CHANGE THE "Y"
SUNRISE THROUGH SUNSET, BY LIGHT OF THE MOON
SEARCHING AT NIGHTTIME, SEARCHING AT NOON
PURSUING WITH PASSION, A PASSABLE LINE
WE MOVE EVER CLOSER! HURRAH!
FORTY-NINE!

> *(**EUGENIA** proudly displays the new forty-nine-letter pangram.)*

EUGENIA. "Back In My Quiet Garden Jolly Zinnias Vie With Frilly Phlox"! Forty-nine letters!

ELLA. Forty-nine! Progress.

NATE. I feel hopeful, yes, most hopeful.

> *(**GWENETTE**, excited and breathless, bursts into the room, paper in hand.)*

GWENETTE. I have one! I have one! Listen, please listen! "Over My Back Wall Grow Sixty Jonquils In Hues Of Azure And Puce"! Fifty-one letters!

> *(There is a moment of stunned silence.)*

ELLA. Lovely but you now must leave Nollop.

GWENETTE. What? Why?

ELLA. You [...] say every illegal letter, multiple times!

NATE. You also have written them.

ELLA. Multiple times!

EUGENIA. And you can't be in possession of that piece of paper.

> *(**GWENETTE** immediately drops the paper.)*

ELLA. Be grateful no LUGs were lying in the bushes.

GWENETTE. *(Flustered, terrified.)* Oh! What was I [...] I haven't been myself since Otto went... I so want life to return to normal. Oh Ella I've lost all [...] common sense.

ELLA. It's all right Mother.

GWENETTE. *(Broken.)* I must leave Enterprise Thirty-two to those more capable. I cannot spare another offense. I am...no more.

ELLA. Rest Mother. You'll be fine.

> *(**GWENETTE** slips quietly away.)*

NATE. So far to go! Only forty sun-to-suns remain.

ELLA. No time to waste...

> *(We now shift to the Towgate home, where **TIMMY** and **GEORGEANNE** conspire. **TIMMY** is now dressed in a miniature version of the LUG uniform, complete with whistle.)*

GEORGEANNE. Oh Timmy! What thrilling success! Together we have shown thirty-three lost lambs the error of their ways, helping them to live once again in the glow of Nollop's light! Plus you are now part of the little league of the LUG. My own precious LUG-a-bug!

TIMMY. I love my whistle.

GEORGEANNE. Mother is grateful for such a son. You are my right arm!

ONE WAY!

ONLY ONE WAY!

> *(We shift to **OTTO**, alone, writing a letter from his new home in Atlantica.)*

OTTO. Dearest Family. I write to you from my new home across the sea. I feel misplaced, a stranger. I do have good news though, my life is happily back on track. My unfortunate tumble from sobriety was thankfully brief. Also I have found a merchant at a local craft store who shows some interest in purchasing my miniatures. I therefore ask a most undeserved favor. Could you please send a sampling of my work? You need only pack things in one of my large shipping boxes.

PACK MY BOX WITH THREE DOZEN TINY CHAIRS

LET'S SAY TEN LITTLE BEDS

A SOFA, NO TWO

A GRANDFATHER CLOCK

AND BEFORE YOU ARE THROUGH...

PACK MY BOX WITH FIVE DOZEN LIQUOR JUGS
IRONIC, I KNOW,
WITH WHAT I'VE BEEN THROUGH
TO PROFIT FROM THOSE
BUT PROFIT I DO

Your husband and father, Otto. This note has been smuggled by a sea merchant I know well which explains why it may smell of shrimp. Also, since this note makes use of forbidden letters hide it my dears. Hide it well!

(We return to the **NOLLOPIANS**. *Their mood has shifted as they have grown weary from their task.)*

NOLLOPIANS.
PENCIL TO PAPER
THE HOURS ARE FEW
TIME RUSHING ON
WITH SO MUCH STILL TO...ACCOMPLISH
FEELING A FAILURE AS SENTENCES STALL.
LOSING ALL PATIENCE, HITTING THE WALL.
WE GRAPPLE, YET STILL NO GRAMMATICAL GRAIL
WE FALTER, WE FLUMMOX, WE FLOP
WE FAIL

(We now see **GWENETTE** *shadowed by an all-seeing* **LUG 1** *in her kitchen.)*

GWENETTE. Ella, unhappy news. I slip. Offense three.
GEORGEANNE RATS ON ME
LUGS HAUL ME IN
PIER SEVEN, AT ONCE
NO MORE MUM
HUG NATE. YOU FIGHT IN OUR HONOR, OUR NAME
OH, ELLA, MY HEART IS HURT

LUG 1. Now! We leave now!

GWENETTE.
LOVE ALWAYS
MUM
FAREWELL FAIR NOLLOP!
FAREWELL!

> (*As* **GWENETTE** *is hauled away we see* **NATE**, **ELLA**, *and* **EUGENIA** *at home.* **ELLA** *holds Gwenette's note.*)

ELLA. Oh Nate, Mother gone. This must stop.

NATE. Yes. Unfortunately we also lose a "U" plus the precious "F" at twelve o'timepiece.

ELLA. "F," "U"...how *apropos*. Perhaps Nollop *IS* taunting us from his grave after all.

NATE. So little time is left. Only twenty sun-to-suns remain.

ELLA. Together we will have fruition.

NATE. Together, yes.

NATE & ELLA.

STARTING ANEW WITH EACH RISE OF THE SUN
PROVING TWO NOGGINS, NICER THAN ONE
WE'RE WILLFUL, WE'RE WILY, WE'RE WINNING THIS WAR

ELLA.

SURPRISE!

NATE.

NO YOU HAVEN'T!

ELLA.

I HAVE!
FORTY-FOUR!

> (**EUGENIA** *proudly reads the new pangram.*)

EUGENIA. "Six Big Devils From Japan Quickly Forgot How To Waltz"! Forty-four letters!

> (*As the triumphant trio celebrate, we move to the town square, where we find a group of defeated* **NOLLOPIANS** *staring up at the statue and the rather sparse, amputated pangram.*)

POPPI. (*A confirmation.*) The "V" has [...] come unattach.

NOLLOPIANS.

TH –UIC– BR–WN –OX ––MPS O–ER THE LA–Y ––G

PENCIL TO PAPER
WITH LITTLE TO SHOW...
TIME GROWING SHORT

SCRATCH OUT "E"
STARE AT "O"...

RUTH.

TONGUES TYING TIGHTER AS LANGUAGE ESCAPES...

PAYTON.

GRUNTING AS WE UN-EVOLVE INTO APES

(At the sound of the illegal "V" usage from **PAYTON,** *a* **LUG** *blows his whistle and hauls him away.)*

RORY.

I'M STRUGGLING

POPPI.

I'M GOING

SHUBERT.

I'M NOTHING

RUTH.

I'M THROUGH

NOLLOPIANS.

IT'S HOPELESS
NO MORE ENTERPRISE THIRTY-TWO

Scene Five

*(A few days later in the Minnow Pea kitchen. The room has been stripped to its barest essentials. At rise, **ELLA** and **EUGENIA** are alone, working. **EUGENIA** is busy counting.)*

ELLA. How many?

EUGENIA. Thirty-six letters! Only four letters away! Mister Nate will be so surprised!

ELLA. Yes. You are the best helper.

EUGENIA. We should keep working. We only have a few days left till the deadline.

ELLA. No, rest a bit. I must see to our supper.

EUGENIA. Something sure does smell good.

ELLA. It's the same [...] unhappy soup again. I'm not sure how much more stretching it will go.

EUGENIA. Well, I like it Miss Ella, truly.

ELLA. You are a tiny liar. It is not enough to [...] sustain a growing girl. You are hungry, yes?

EUGENIA. A little, I suppose.

*(The two are interrupted by **NATE**'s exuberant entrance.)*

NATE. Greetings my angel girls! I come with news! Plus a present!

EUGENIA. A present?

NATE. *(Producing a hidden package.)* I possess lime gelatin!

EUGENIA. *(Thrilled.)* Yay!

*(**ELLA** hands the package to **EUGENIA**.)*

ELLA. Please put this in the other room so we can prepare it in a bit, yes?

EUGENIA. Okay. You need some "grown-up" time, right?

ELLA. Yes.

*(**EUGENIA** exits. **NATE**'s mood becomes serious.)*

NATE. Oh Ella, town is [...] ghost place. Nightmare... I saw LUGs shooting people...horrible...

ELLA. But you bring gelatin. How?

NATE. I locate nice man who exchange one can stew tomato. Happy news: he also has gasoline to run generator.

ELLA. Yes! So tomorrow you exchange something else!

NATE. *(Surveying.)* So little remains. We exchange almost all.

ELLA. We still possess many tins of green beans. I'm so [...] nauseous with green beans.

NATE. I also possess not-so-nice news. More tiles topple.

ELLA. How many?

NATE. Three plus two.

ELLA. All at once?

> **(EUGENIA** *has entered, quietly listening.)*

NATE. Gone now, "T," "R," "C," "B," "H."

> *(The pangram now reads "T–e –ui–– –r–wn –ox ––mps O–e– –he la–y ––g.")*

ELLA. When go?

NATE. Tonight. Sun-to-sun cusp as usual.

EUGENIA. Midnight.

ELLA. No more unhappy news! Enough! I possess nice news!

EUGENIA. We have news! Wonderful, exciting news!

NATE. Oh really! Tell!

ELLA. *(Giving* **EUGENIA** *permission.)* Go on...

EUGENIA. *(Reading.)* "Quick, Weave Eight Dozen Nubby Flax Jumpers." Thirty-six letters!

NATE. So close to our goal now!

EUGENIA. Miss Ella came up with it right out of the blue!

NATE. My girls are so smart!

> *(There is a knock on the door.* **NATE** *answers to find* **GEORGEANNE** *and* **TIMMY. GEORGEANNE**

carries a large basket filled with baked goods and vegetables from her garden. **TIMMY** *is in full LUG-a-bug uniform.)*

GEORGEANNE. *(Humble, kind.)* Is it an opportune time to call?

ELLA. *(With sarcasm.)* Sure, why not.

GEORGEANNE. I come in the niceness spirit with happy unity.

ELLA. Happy unity? You sent our mothers away! You call that "niceness spirit"?

GEORGEANNE. *(Remaining calm, simply.)* Your mothers sent your mothers away. I was merely the unhappy instrument to Nollop's wise will. Still this is not time to share [...] apart-ness. I come with a large heart.

ELLA. Really. It still seems small to me.

GEORGEANNE. Also with yummies! I possess present with necessary sustenance. Eugenia must get nourishment. Ella, stop with the set-in-your-ways. Please...

> *(After a glance to* **EUGENIA,** *who is indeed eyeing the food with much interest,* **ELLA** *concedes.)*

ELLA. *(Taking the basket.)* Only to Eugenia to eat. We not eat.

NATE. *(Softening a bit.)* Much appreciation to you.

GEORGEANNE. Not me! All niceties are Nollop courtesy. All hail to Nollop! One way, only one way!

ELLA. *(Disgusted, pushing basket away.)* No, not one way! Many ways! We no accept! We return it.

GEORGEANNE. *(Strongly.)* Ella! Stop the unwiseness. Nollop will win. Enterprise Thirty-two is going nowhere.

ELLA. Oh really, going nowhere? Well I have news for you.

[MUSIC NO. 14A "36! / NATE'S ARREST"]

We are now at thirty-six!

EUGENIA. Only four letters to go!

ELLA. *(Directly to **GEORGEANNE**.)*
    YOU SEE WE AREN'T GOING TO STOP, NOT NOW!
    WE'LL SEE OUR WAY THROUGH THIS SOMEWAY,
        SOMEHOW!
    WE'LL STOP ALL THIS MESS, WE'RE SO CLOSE TO SUCCESS!
    NOT LONG UNTIL
    WE WIN! WE WILL!

NATE. *(Overjoyed, unbridled.)* Oh Ella! I love you so much!

    (An immediate, hushed silence.)

EUGENIA. *(Scared.)* No, Mister Nate! You can't say "love"...

TIMMY. And you said it loud and clear! Illegal letter usage!

    *(**TIMMY** looks to his mother, awaiting her cue.
    ELLA pleads directly with **GEORGEANNE**.)*

ELLA. No, please. Not Nate I pray you.

GEORGEANNE. *(Unrelenting.)* One way, only one way.

    *(And with that, a cold and steady
    GEORGEANNE nods to **TIMMY**, who
    immediately blows his horrid whistle. The
    front door bursts open with a pair of ever-
    ready **LUGS**, who grab **NATE** and toss him
    into the dark, followed by **GEORGEANNE** and
    TIMMY. **ELLA** stands framed in the doorway,
    clutching little **EUGENIA**.)*

ELLA. *(Wounded.)* Nate, no!

Scene Six

[MUSIC NO. 15 "YOU'LL SEE"]

(We return to Pier Seven. We find **NATE**, **ELLA**, *and* **EUGENIA** *isolated on the docks.)*

NATE. Ella, listen to me. Look at me.

ELLA. Nate, no.

NATE. We only have a few minutes left and then I must leave.

ELLA. No, no go! I go too! Please!

NATE. Ella, no. You can do this!

ELLA. No! Me minus you is too small.

      (She struggles to tell him what she cannot.)

I must say more to you... I possess no letters to say what I want!

NATE. *(Forcefully.)*

ELLA, STOP!
YOU'RE NOT THINKING CLEARLY
ELLA, STOP!
YOU'VE FORGOTTEN HOW NEAR WE
ARE TO OUR GOAL
TO SEEING THIS WHOLE
NIGHTMARE THROUGH
ELLA, STOP!
AND LISTEN TO WHAT I'M SAYING TO YOU

SOON THIS WILL ALL BE ENDED
YOU'LL SEE
SOON, ALL THAT'S BROKEN, MENDED
YOU'LL SEE
SOME THINGS ARE CERTAIN
SOME THINGS YOU TRUST
SOME THINGS ARE JUST MEANT TO BE
SOME THINGS, LIKE YOU AND ME
YOU'LL SEE

LOOK AT ME ELLA. LOOK IN MY EYES
I'LL HEAR WHAT YOU CANNOT SAY
WE'LL SAVE WORDS FOR ANOTHER DAY

I'M WITH YOU ELLA
INSIDE YOUR HEART
ELLA, NOW IT'S UP TO YOU
DON'T BE SCARED
YOU CAN SEE THIS THROUGH
YOU'LL SEE!

  (**LUG 1** *starts with his list of names.*)

LUG 1.
SHUBERT GREENLY!

NATE. *(To* **EUGENIA.**) You take care of Ella for me.

EUGENIA. I will, Mister Nate!

LUG 1.
RORY O'LOOLEY!

NATE. Farewell, my girls! I love you so!

LUG 1.
NATHANIEL WARREN!

NATE. I love you, Ella!

ELLA. *(A struggle.)*
I TOO! YOU NATE!
I TOO YOU!
(A frantic command to **EUGENIA.**) Say! Say too! Now!

  (**EUGENIA** *passionately cries out after* **NATE.**)

EUGENIA.
SHE LOVES YOU, MISTER NATE!

ELLA.
YES!

EUGENIA.
ELLA LOVES NATE!

LUG 1. You must go now!

NATE.	**ELLA.**	
FAREWELL MY	SAY! YES!	
GIRLS		**EUGENIA.**
		SHE LOVES
		YOU!
		SHE LOVES
		YOU!

NATE.	ELLA.	EUGENIA.
FAREWELL!	NO!	SHE LOVES YOU!

(As **NATE** *is pulled away, the lights fade on a broken* **ELLA** *and* **EUGENIA.***)*

Scene Seven

[MUSIC NO. 15A "CHILDREN, DEPORTED / SCENE SEVEN"]

(**LUG 2** *is making an official announcement.*)

LUG 2.

NEWS: OUR HIGH GROUP RULERS

OUR NOLLOP HOME IS NOW NO SPOT
TO RAISE A YOUNGSTER!
SO *ALL* YOUNGSTERS ARE NOW NO-NO!
ALL YOUNGSTERS MUST NOW GO!
NOLLOP WISE TO WANT IT SO
YOUNGSTERS GO NOW!

> (*We are back in the Minnow Pea home.* **ELLA** *is quiet, deeply saddened. A concerned* **EUGENIA** *watches her for a bit before speaking.*)

ELLA. No more...

EUGENIA. Miss Pea, they will be here soon to take me away.

ELLA. Why must I lose you? Why are they...?

EUGENIA. Because they know that you are getting close to winning. They think that they can stop you by taking me away but you are stronger and smarter than they are. You have work to do!

ELLA. How? No you?

EUGENIA.

PENCIL TO PAPER
COME ON MISS PEA, TRY!

You only have two days left...

EVEN WITHOUT ME, YOU CAN!

ELLA.

NO SEE WHY

EUGENIA.

BECAUSE WHERE WE LIVE IS A PLACE LIKE NO OTHER
DO IT FOR NATE, FOR YOUR FATHER AND MOTHER
LISTEN MISS PEA FIGURE OUT WHAT TO DO
YOU HAVE TO FOR EV'RYONE'S COUNTING ON YOU

*(We immediately shift to a split stage: the Towgate home, where **GEORGEANNE**, in a state of extreme agitation, paces the floor, ranting as a confused **TIMMY** looks on, and the Minnow Pea home, where **LUG 2** is taking **EUGENIA** away as a helpless **ELLA** observes.)*

GEORGEANNE.

ALL HAIL TO NOLLOP
ALL HAIL TO NOLLOP
ALL HAIL TO NOLLOP
WHO IS ALWAYS RIGHT!

ELLA.

NO!
NO GO!
NO!

*(We leave **ELLA** alone and focus on the Towgate home.)*

GEORGEANNE. *(Seething.)* Take my Timmy away! Never! Fools! Blind, blind fools!

TIMMY.

(Confused, scared.)
Mother, you're saying illegal letters! Stop! Where's my whistle? My whistle!

GEORGEANNE.

Separate us!

After all we've done? Our accomplishments?

Never!

GEORGEANNE. *(Taking the whistle.)* Timmy, no more whistle. They will be here soon to try and take you. Quick help Mother! Lock the door, shutter the windows! Quickly!

[MUSIC NO. 16 "LITTLE ISLAND – REPRISE"]

*(The two move with great purpose, locking doors, closing blinds, as **GEORGEANNE** continues her rant.)*

(A painful, insane scream.) BETRAYED!
(She blows the whistle.) Offense number one!
(A second howl.) TRAPPED!
(Again the whistle.) Number two!
(A final blow of the whistle.) FINISHED! Offense number three!

(Her work finished, **GEORGEANNE** *pulls* **TIMMY** *close to her in a large chair. A small side table holds a lovely crystal pitcher and glass.)*

Timmy, come here and sit with me. You see I have sinned, broken the letter laws, and so I am banished from this misguided island and must leave. You want to come with me don't you?

TIMMY. Yes. But where are we going? To Atlantica?

GEORGEANNE. Atlantica? Never. That godless world is a worse hell than the one we are already in. No, sadly this world has no home for us. We have only one choice. It is time for us to go where forgiveness from Nollop awaits. Before this day is over we will be at the foot of Nollop's throne!

TIMMY. Where is that? How do we get there?

(She fills the glass and offers it to **TIMMY.***)*

GEORGEANNE. Here, drink this, my love.

TIMMY. Why? What is it?

GEORGEANNE. *(Comforting.)* Shhhh…

DRINK THIS NOW
DO AS I SAY
YOU HAVE TO TRUST
FOR IT'S THE ONLY WAY
GO TO SLEEP
AND DON'T BE SCARED
MOTHER'S HERE
AND MOTHER IS PREPARED

CLOSE YOUR EYES
IT'S TIME THAT YOU REST
YES, TIMMY, THIS IS
OUR FINAL TEST

WE'VE ALWAYS BEEN ALONE
THAT'S CLEARLY BEEN THE CASE
BUT NOW WE'LL WAKE UP IN A
FAR MORE UNDERSTANDING PLACE

TOGETHER, YOU AND I

YES, IT'S TIME TO SAY GOODBYE

TO THIS
SAD, DECEITFUL,
AND MISGUIDED,
UNDERHANDEDLY
ONE-SIDED,
DOUBLE-CROSSING,
AND BACKSTABBING,
CRUEL, BETRAYING,
OFFSPRING GRABBING,
LITTLE ISLAND

> *(She take out a small revolver from beneath the chair and places it against her temple, a lifeless* **TIMMY** *across her lap.)*

FLOATING...
DRIFTING...
LOST...
IN THE...

> *(There is a deafening gunshot as the lights plunge to blackness.)*

Scene Eight

[MUSIC NO. 17 "LMNOP"]

(From the shadows we hear **ELLA***'s cries.)*

ELLA.

NO!
NO MO!
NO! NO!

*(**LUG 2** is seen making an announcement.)*

LUG 2.

NEWS! OUR HIGH GROUP RULERS!

MORE LETTERS GONE!
ONLY LMNOP REMAIN!
START NOW!
ONLY LMNOP

*(It is the dead of night. **ELLA** has taken out illegal letters she has secreted away and is going through them, reliving the recent events. She is at turns defeated, exhausted, and at times almost deliriously happy, strangely giddy.)*

ELLA.

LMNOP
LMNOP
LMNOP
LMNOP!

NO MO NOLLOP POMP!
NO MO NOLLOP POO POO!
NO MO PLOP! PLOP! PLOP!
NO MO LMNOP!
PO, PO LMNOP
NO MO

*(She pulls out a recent letter from **NATE**.)*

NATE.

I'M WITH YOU ELLA

INSIDE YOUR HEART
ELLA, NOW IT'S UP TO YOU
DON'T BE SCARED
YOU CAN SEE THIS THROUGH
YOU'LL SEE

  (*A saddened* **ELLA** *hugs herself tightly, rocking back and forth.*)

ELLA.

LOO LOO!
NO MO LOO LOO!

  (*She pulls out her mother's goodbye letter.*)

GWENETTE.	**ELLA.**
Ella. Unhappy news.	O MOM
Offense three.	O, O, O!

GWENETTE.

YOU FIGHT IN OUR HONOR
OUR NAME
OH ELLA MY HEART IS HURT
LOVE ALWAYS...MOM!

  (**ELLA** *now takes out a recent letter from her father.*)

OTTO.

Dearest family, I write to	**ELLA.**
you from across the sea...	POP POP!

OTTO.

LET'S SAY TEN LITTLE BEDS
A SOFA, NO TWO
A GRANDFATHER CLOCK
AND BEFORE YOU ARE THROUGH...
PACK MY BOX WITH FIVE DOZEN
LIQUOR JUGS
IRONIC, I KNOW
WITH WHAT I'VE BEEN...

  (*Sensing something,* **ELLA** *rereads a part of the letter.*)

OTTO.

    PACK MY BOX WITH FIVE
        DOZEN
    LIQUOR JUGS ...   **ELLA.**

                Pop! Pop!

    (A realization growing stronger, she reads again.)

    PACK MY BOX WITH FIVE
        DOZEN
    LIQUOR JUGS...   LO LO LO LO LO LO LO LO
                                     LO LO LO

    (Again, as she simultaneously hums a familiar tune.)

    PACK MY BOX WITH FIVE   LO LO LO LO LO LO LO LO
        DOZEN   LO LO LO
    LIQUOR JUGS...

    (Elated, throwing caution aside, she furiously scribbles the words.)

ELLA.

    PACK MY BOX WITH FIVE DOZEN LIQUOR JUGS!

    Thirty-two letters!

    *(The door opens and a pair of **LUGS** enter, whistles blowing, fingers pointed at **ELLA**.)*

    BLOW EVERY WHISTLE!
    WAKE ALL FROM THEIR SLEEP!
    AND TELL OUR DEAR COUNCIL
    TO READ THIS AND WEEP!
    THE CHALLENGE IS MET
    AND THIS WAR HAS BEEN WON!
    AT LAST
    AND FOREVERMORE
    IT IS DONE!

    *(The **LUGS** retreat as **ELLA** moves downstage, composing a letter.)*

[MUSIC NO. 18 "ACT TWO FINALE"]

ELLA. Dearest Mother, Father, and beloved Nate. I have stumbled upon the answer to our prayers. A simple sentence, created quite accidentally by you Pop, and only seconds before the deadline. The good news has spread quickly and Nollopians have already started to return to our beautiful shores. So, hurry and please, please, please... Come home!

(The **NOLLOPIANS** *return home, singing with full-throated jubilation.)*

NOLLOPIANS.	GWENETTE, OTTO, SHUBERT, NATE, PEABODY & AGNES.
WELCOME HOME FAIR NOLLOP!	WELCOME HOME FAIR NOLLOP!
	I AM HOME FAIR NOLLOP
NOLLOP IS OUR HOME!	I'M HOME
IT IS OVER AT LAST!	IT IS OVER AT LAST!
WE ARE HOME!	WE ARE HOME!
DAUGHTERS, HUG YOUR MOTHERS	DAUGHTERS HUG YOUR MOTHERS, SISTERS, FATHERS,
BROTHERS	BROTHERS
ALL ARE HOME!	I'M HOME

(We immediately segue to a town hall meeting led by **GWENETTE.** *The mood is solemn and respectful.)*

GWENETTE. Dearest Nollopians! I, Gwenette Minnow Pea, call this meeting of the Nollopian Common Sense Council to order. As acting president I vow to govern fairly and compassionately with checks and balances firmly in place to ensure that the likes of our last misguided Council can never poison our fair shores again. One month into our rebuilding I am happy to report that the library has been restocked and businesses have been returned to their rightful owners. Also, the poor abused statue of Nollop that once stood in our town square has been removed. The votes to determine what should take its place have been tallied and it is not without a bit of pride that I announce the winner, in a landslide, is a statue of my own daughter Ella crouched by the light of a single lantern commemorating her formidable courage and ultimate victory. The statue will be...

ELLA. *(Stepping in, interrupting.)* Mother, I'm sorry...if I may...

GWENETTE. And it appears, unsurprisingly, that she has something to say. Ella...

ELLA. *(Sweetly.)* Thanks Mom.

(Addressing the crowd.) Dearest friends and fellow Nollopians...

THIS HONOR FOR ME
UPON WHICH YOU'VE DECIDED
IS LOVELY IN THOUGHT
BUT SOMEWHAT MISGUIDED
ALL THAT OCCURRED I MUST HUMBLY CONFESS
WAS A RANDOM EVENT. NOTHING MORE, NOTHING LESS
AND MISPLACED DEVOTION CAN LEAD TO REGRET
A NEWLY LEARNED LESSON THAT WE SHOULD NOT
    FORGET

SO THANKS FOR THE OFFER
BUT I MUST DECLINE
FOR THE GLORY IS OURS
AND NOT MERELY MINE
SO LET US PAY TRIBUTE TO ALL THOSE WHO TRIED
WHO SACRIFICED BRAVELY
WHO SUFFERED
WHO DIED

*(**NATE** steps up to stand at **ELLA**'s side.)*

NATE. Ella and I do, however, have an idea for a monument. One to be dedicated to all Nollopians past, present, and yet to come.

ELLA. A sculpture depicting a large box filled with moonshine jugs, piled high, corks popping, spirits pouring, representing our glorious language...words upon words, toppling over, conversation freely flowing forever and ever without end.

ALL. Forever and ever without end!

ELLA.
> WE STAND HERE NOW
> THE BATTLE WON

NATE & ELLA.
> THE STORM HAS PASSED
> A NEW DAY HAS BEGUN

GWENETTE & OTTO.
> ALTHOUGH OUR SCARS
> IN TIME WILL FADE

ELLA, NATE, GWENETTE & OTTO.
> WE WON'T FORGET
> THE PRICE WE'VE PAID

AGNES & PEABODY.
> WITH LESSONS THAT WILL
> HOPEFULLY LAST

AGNES, PEABODY, RUTH & SHUBERT.
> WE LOOK AHEAD
> YET HONOR THE PAST

AGNES & GWENETTE.
> UNITED, FRIEND TO FRIEND

OTTO.
> AND STRONGER THAN BEFORE

NATE & ELLA.
> WE'LL FACE WHATEVER CHALLENGES
> THE FUTURE HOLDS IN STORE

ALL.
> AND WE'LL LIVE EACH BLESSED DAY
> IN OUR OWN RED-LETTER WAY
>
> ON THIS
> RATHER SMALL, BUT STILL IMPRESSIVE
> ANTIQUATED
> YET PROGRESSIVE
> PACIFISTIC

WHILE VICTORIOUS
QUITE UNIQUE
AND SIMPLY GLORIOUS
LITTLE ISLAND

WOMEN.

CALLED NOLLOP   **MEN.**
NOLLOP   WE LIVE IN NOLLOP
NOLLOP   OUR HOME IS NOLLOP

(The happy and contented **NOLLOPIANS** *go about their day, and with a contented sigh, the play is over.)*

The End

www.ingramcontent.com/pod-product-compliance
Lightning Source LLC
Chambersburg PA
CBHW070336120726
47909CB00008B/2701